MW01047241

One Desirable Man

Written by: Craig Felipe Simpson

Dedicated to all the people worldwide who have suffered greatly because of injustice.

This book was inspired by the wrongful arrest of Juan Catalan and the wrongful arrest and conviction of Steven Avery.
This book is a work of fiction and is not meant to depict any specific case past or present. Any similarity with any past or present case or person should be considered a coincidence.

To see other publications by Craig Felipe Simpson visit:
www.craigfelipe-artist.com

Chapter 1 - Code Red

It's the first week of December 2021, and all over the world troubling reports are coming in of sudden deaths. The deaths increase at a blistering pace, causing cancelled flights, forced landings of airplanes, and overall chaos in the worldwide economy. The president of the United States calls an emergency meeting in the Situation Room, and on Friday morning all her top advisors are present. "Ok, can someone tell me what the hell is going on?"

Everyone looks at the Surgeon General who rises to his feet and begins a PowerPoint presentation.

"Two days after Thanksgiving, hospitals all over the country began to report far more cases than usual of heart attacks, or high blood pressure. All patients eventually died or are expected to die, because we have no idea what is causing this to happen. We thought that it was a case of food poisoning since the incidents increased sharply after Thanksgiving, however, we had to dismiss that theory."

"Why?" The President snaps.

"Because we realized that only males were dying. In fact, so many men have died and gotten sick that emergency healthcare is a problem. Many first responders have taken ill and some have already died, we're at a crisis level right now."

There is a moment of silence as everyone looks around the room nervously.

The silence is broken as the Surgeon General continues: "I have spoken to the other advisors and respective Secretaries, and we have a plan that we'd like you to approve immediately Mrs. President."

"What's the plan?" The President asks.

"We would like you to halt all travel to and from the United States, and prohibit all males from leaving their homes, with the exception of first responders and medical personnel. However, they will be required to wear a mask." The President looks at the Surgeon General with her mouth wide open: "Are you kidding me?"

"I kid you not Mrs. President, this is a national and probably an international emergency. In fact, on my way here I was looking over some new reports, and based on those reports I would suggest you declare a state of emergency. The bodies are piling up so quickly that there is no way we will be able to do an autopsy on everyone. I want to ask all the States to save the body of every thousandth victim, and cremate the others as soon as possible."

Everyone looks at the President as she looks around the room nervously. During the presidential debates, she was accused of not being a strong enough leader who would be able to make the tough decisions, so without thinking too much she says: "Let's make it happen. Notify the media outlets, there will be a press conference at midday!" As soon as the President speaks, the chairman of the Joint Chiefs of Staff starts to breathe heavily as he loosens his collar. He stands up to try and fill his lungs with air but instead falls to the ground. All hell breaks loose as everyone scampers out of the room.

It is now late December, every single man who was in the Situation Room with the president that day has died. There was a press conference and the state of emergency was declared, but none of those measures could prevent the wave of death that swooped across the entire planet. Nations all over the world implemented the same policies that were implemented in the United States. As the death rate climbed, nurses and doctors limited themselves to taking blood and tissue samples before cremating the bodies. In many countries, especially the poorer ones, people still buried their men the traditional way. No one celebrated Christmas, birthdays, nothing! The New Year brought more deaths and more funerals.

It's now the second week of February, and every news report shows the President of the United States touring communities all over the country as they lay their fallen men to rest. The State of The Union speech is just around the corner, and the President wants to get a firsthand look at the situation before speaking to the American people.

The President is so deeply affected by the death and despair of the people that she ends up cancelling the State of The Union speech. She then orders her advisors to work twice as hard to find out what has happened.

Chapter 2 – A Clue

As the month of April 2022 rolls around, a meeting is scheduled in the Situation Room and the President, who is now a widow, walks in.

Everyone rises as the President walks in and stands in front of her chair at the head of the table.

"Please be seated. As many of you may have heard, I lost my husband to this evil scourge over the weekend. He was the last remaining male in America. He was hidden away for weeks in a sterilized room, in fact, I was the only one allowed to go inside to see him… after taking a bath, sterilizing every crevice of my body, and waiting 12 hours in quarantine. I need to know how this happened, I NEED ANSWERS PEOPLE!" She shouted, as she slammed her fist on the desk and dropped into her chair. As the President settles in her chair with her dark glasses still covering her puffy red eyes, the new Surgeon General rises to her feet and establishes a video link with the CDC office in Atlanta.

"Mrs. President, I'm sure you know Marlene Samuels, head of the CDC."

"Hi Marlene, how are you?"

"I'm hanging on in there Mrs. President, it's hard, but I'm hanging on."

"Talk to me Marlene, what did you find?"

"Last year, when this outbreak started, we thought it was food poisoning. After that didn't pan out we realized it was probably a pathogen, but we couldn't identify the pathogen, and even blood and tissue samples from victims did not provide any clues. However, after comparing several blood and tissues samples from here in the USA and after reviewing the data submitted by my counterparts in other countries, I think I've been able to identify the culprit. Now, Mrs. President, I'm sure you've heard of good bacteria?"

"Yes, those are the bacteria that live in our gut and help us to digest food correct?"

"Correct Mrs. President, but there is also good bacteria on our skin, eyelids, inside the mouth etc. Good bacteria helps to break down sweat and they carry out a multitude of other useful functions. We believe this plague is being caused by a genetically modified 'good' bacteria."

"How is that so?" the president asks as she removes her sunglasses and sits up in her chair.

"Well, when we analyzed tissue and blood samples from victims, we came across good bacteria that we would normally find in the human body. That of course

didn't raise any alarms because it was normal. Even when we started to analyze those bacteria more carefully under an electron microscope, we didn't notice anything suspicious. However, when we got some samples from Africa and Asia from some partially decomposed corpses, we noticed that spores had formed?"
"Spores?" The President asks.
"Yes, so basically, unlike a virus that needs a living host to live in and survive, bacteria can survive for short periods even on a surface like a desk, chair, counter etc. And if the surface is moist, it can survive even longer. However, they can't survive very long under harsh conditions, unless they have the ability to form a spore, and not all bacteria have that ability. So to form a spore, a bacterium will strip itself down to a more simplified form that can lie dormant for a long time. Some spores have the ability to survive thousands of years, but apparently this spore will only survive about four weeks before it starts to die completely. The thing that is working to this bacteria's advantage is that it is spread easily through human contact. It can survive and reproduce on your skin, but not under sunlight. It then moves inside the body where it multiplies and appears in body fluids such as saliva etcetera. If you sneeze it will survive in the air for a long time and then someone else can breathe it into their nostrils where it will multiply. The body sees it as good bacteria, so there is no immune response. It will continue to multiply and spread, even when it is causing damage to the host."

"Marlene" the President says as she puts her sunglasses back on and looks up at the giant TV screen "are you saying that I unwittingly killed my husband?"
There is a deafening silence in the room as everyone looks up at the TV screen. Marlene takes a deep breath and begins to speak. "Mrs. President, millions of women on this planet have unknowingly passed on the bacteria to their husbands and boyfriends through sexual contact, but it doesn't stop there. Even a brief kiss on the cheek has allowed women to pass it on to their sons, daughters, and other relatives. Women serve only as carriers and transmitters of the disease, while men have the added role of being victims."
"But why the hell is this bacteria only killing men?" The President shouts, as she clenches her fist and shakes with anger.
Again, everyone looks at the huge TV screen, and Marlene who is now looking like a clueless teenager says: "Mrs. President, that we don't know. What we do know is that the bacteria seems to feed off blood sugar and the waste matter that it generates damages the kidneys and raises blood pressure to fatal levels, causing most men to die of heart failure, a stroke, and or kidney failure."

There is another huge pause and silence as the President looks down at the table and shakes her head. Looking up, she can see that everyone is looking at her. "Okay, here is what we do. Send the information regarding the bacteria to every single country in the world. Let's see if we can stop this bacteria before it kills every single man on this planet. Otherwise, the human race will not survive another one hundred years.

Chapter 3 – Chaos

It's now a month since that video conference with Marlene, and the President is travelling on Air Force One on her way to Atlanta, Georgia. The world is in chaos as the male population is wiped out. In African and Middle Eastern countries, the news about the bacteria was met with suspicion. Many accused America and Great Britain of trying to kill off black people, or kill off Muslims. Instead of quarantining their men, the leaders proposed having more babies. The bacteria spread fast, and in less than six months Africa and the Middle East did not have any men remaining. The news regarding the bacteria arrived in developed countries too late. In most countries, the military and police were able to keep social order. However, in some rural areas and areas of conflict, young women and girls formed gangs to guarantee their survival, as well as access to food and other resources.

With the worldwide male population now at zero, burials have slowed down greatly, but now they are burying women. Many elderly women are dying from stress and a lack of doctors to attend to their healthcare needs. Construction has come to a halt because there is no need for new housing or factory space right now. Countries where women were prohibited from working outside the home or going to University are the hardest hit. Many women have died from job related accidents, and certain trades are suffering, because many women are too scared of the risks and dangers they have to face on the job.

As soon as Air Force One lands in Georgia, a VIP helicopter takes the President to the CDC headquarters, escorted by two Apache military helicopters. As soon as the President lands she steps out and begins to walk briskly across the lawn as the two Apaches circle overhead.

The Secret Service agents guide the president through the hallways to a large conference room where she is taken to a leather office chair at the end of a table. At the other end of the table is a huge TV screen, and as a member of her entourage connects a laptop to the TV, the President says: "Good morning everyone. Last week at this time I thought all males on this planet had died off. Today, I can say for a certainty that this is not true. As some of you may know, there are a few small tribes in South America in the Amazon jungle. The Peruvian and Brazilian governments have had laws in place for decades that make it illegal to come in contact with these tribes, who have a history of violence and aggression towards outsiders. As you can see in these satellite pictures on the screen, the men in those tribes are alive and doing well. This next set of pictures shows a tribe living on an Island in the Indian Ocean. They have a history of being violent towards outsiders, and for decades the Indian government has made it illegal to approach the Island. All those photos were taken by our satellites, however, this last photo was taken by a Russian satellite. It's a black man dressed in white shorts and a white T-shirt and he's wearing sunglasses. Marlene, would you like to comment on this?"

There is a loud gasp in the room as everyone turns and looks at the head of the CDC. "Mrs. President, that information is extremely classified, are you sure you want me to talk about that?"

"Everyone in this room has top secret security clearance, and are well aware of the consequences if they leak this information." This the President says as she slowly glares at each and every person in the room, including the two bodyguards who are standing on each side of her. She returns her gaze to Marlene who takes that as her cue to start giving her explanation.

"The gentleman you saw in the picture is Tyrone Marshall, a convicted rapist and killer here in the state of Georgia. After the Supreme Court refused to hear his case, he was scheduled for execution on January 31 of this year. When the outbreak started, prison populations were the first ones to die out, but Mr. Marshall survived…".

"How did that happen?" The President asks.

"We have no idea" Marlene responds, "we believe the prisoners on death row were the last ones to be infected, but all of them died except him. Truth be told, he was in solitary confinement because he had an infection, and he did not have the same meals as the other prisoners. The only thing he would eat is chicken soup made by his mother, which she brought every day…"

"WHY THE HELL DID I HAVE TO FIND THIS OUT FROM THE RUSSIANS?" The President yells, "I FELT LIKE A FOOL DENYING THIS, ONLY TO BE HANDED A SATELLITE PHOTO OF A BURLY BLACK MAN SITTING ON THE ROOF OF A WING OF THE CDC BUILDING SIPPING A PINA COLADA!"

"They could tell it was a Pina Colada from a satellite photo? Dang! They're good!" The President turns and glares at the person who made the comment, just before Marlene intervenes. "My apologies Mrs. President, this is my assistant Trudy, as you can see she is very young and impressionable. I take full responsibility for hiding Mr. Marshall from not just you, but the public in general. I saw where this was headed and I considered it a security risk to let anyone else know about Mr. Marshall, in fact, his family thinks he is dead…"

"What?" The President asks, with her eyes wide open, "you told his family that he was dead?"

"Well, we didn't actually say he was dead, they drew that conclusion and we didn't correct them."

Marlene shrugs her shoulders like a teenager caught in a lie as the President allows her head to fall into her palms on the table. Everyone in the room looks around uneasily, except for the two Secret Service Agents whose expressions are hidden behind their sunglasses.

Looking up, the President says: "The Russians have given us seven days to provide an explanation before they go public with that photo…"

"Those bitches are mean" Trudy remarks, but she quickly apologizes for her outburst as Marlene elbows her in the side.

The President slowly looks away from Trudy as she continues: "I am going to have the Secret Service bring his mother here to see him, make sure they have no problems getting in here."

"Yes ma'am" Marlene responds.

Chapter 4 – The Offer

It is three days before the Russian deadline. Tyrone has already met with his mother who was asked not to reveal his whereabouts, or identify him as her son. Now he is alone in a conference room waiting, and then the moment arrives. A woman dressed in a pants suit walks into the conference room, followed by four burly female corrections officers. She sits down at the opposite end of the conference table from Tyrone and then asks the officers to wait outside the conference room.

"Good morning Mr. Marshall, how are you?"

"I'm good thanks".

"Well my name is…"

"Penny Wright, the woman who sent me to prison. How nice of you to drop by, how long has it been, ten years?"

"Actually Mr. Marshall, a jury of your peers sent you to prison, I wasn't even lead counsel. I was a young prosecutor playing second fiddle to the man who prosecuted you, now he's dead, so I get to meet with you. Let me cut to the chase here, you are scheduled to be executed, and although that execution has been delayed, it has not been cancelled. I'm here to make you an offer. There are thousands of women all over the world who are willing to make the sacrifice of carrying your children so that we can guarantee the survival of the human race. If you sign this document agreeing to participate in the program, then we remove the death penalty from your sentence and make it life imprisonment. After the program is complete, you could even go free".

Tyrone smiles and looks her straight in the eyes, but Penny is tough. She's been with the District Attorney's office for ten years, and she has come face to face with some of the meanest criminals in the state of Georgia.

"So first you try to kill me, then you do everything to save my life, and now you try to pimp me out to the world in exchange for my freedom. Do you think I'm an idiot? Momma didn't raise no fool, so go back to whoever sent you and tell them that I need a retrial, because I'm innocent."

With that comment, Tyrone rises to his feet and leaves the room. He is supposed to be on death row, but he has a CDC guest security badge that allows him access to specific areas only, including his makeshift living area. He even has a cell phone and a 75 inch LED TV. He now talks to his mother every day and he watches TV.

He goes to the gym daily and his refrigerator is always stocked with fresh food, but now his mother wants to bring him a home cooked meal every two days.

Tyrone had not turned back to look at Penny as he left the conference room, but she was later joined by Marlene, and together they walked to the secure conference room where they are now speaking to the President.
"So basically Mrs. President, he's obviously not going to discuss this matter until he gets a retrial because he swears he's innocent."
"So what are you waiting on? Make it happen!"
"Mrs. President, I can't make a retrial happen, the Georgia Supreme Court upheld his conviction, and the US Supreme refused to hear his case, he's on death row right now."
"Miss Wright, you are so wrong. Remember, I'm a lawyer also. As a prosecutor you can look into the case again with fresh eyes, and it would help if you got his original attorney involved."
"How would I find her?"
"Why do I have to do everyone's job for them?" the President asks, as she looks around in disgust. "She's the attorney of record, look up her bar number on the docket then check with the State Bar of Georgia to see where she's practicing right now! Never mind, I already have the information. She left the Public Defender's office a year after his conviction and started working with an attorney in Valdosta. I'll be addressing the nation tonight, so make sure you, the Governor, and the DA are all on the same page." The transmission ends and the women look at each other before getting to work.

At 9:00 PM Eastern time, everyone is tuned in to their TVs. The entire world is watching, not just English speaking countries. Interpreters have been hired in non-English speaking countries to simultaneously translate the President's address, and at exactly 9:00 PM she begins her speech.
"Ladies… and gentleman. Some of you already knew what this address would be about, but if you didn't know before, I'm sure my opening words gave you a clue. Many of you were told that the only males remaining on this planet were in a few isolated tribes in South America and one island in the Indian Ocean. I am here to tell you that we have one here in the United States."
There is a loud gasp all over the world as millions of women and girls look at each other wild-eyed.

"Now, I know what many of you are thinking, but please bear in mind that this person is a convicted rapist and murderer who was scheduled to be executed. In addition, we need to keep him in isolation for the time being until we are sure that he will not get infected and die. As soon as I have more information I will schedule another press conference."

As the press conference ends and the president walks away, attorney's and legal experts from all over the world begin to debate the issue. Tyrone, who is watching from his room, smiles then laughs out loud. It's the first time he has laughed in over ten years. That same night Tyrone receives a text message, there is a meeting at 2:00pm the next day with his former attorney and the DA. This a meeting that Tyrone has dreamed of for the past ten years, but in the end he never thought it possible

Chapter 5 – Let's Deal

At 1:30pm the next day, there is a knock on Tyrone's door, and he opens it to see his former Public Defender, Jennifer O'Riley. The years have been kind to her, she looks the same as she did ten years ago, but she has lost a little weight. About 5 feet 9 inches and change, red hair and bluish green eyes. Even if no one told you, her Irish roots are obvious.

"Miss O'Riley, long time."

"Yes, it has been a long time."

"Do you work close by? It appears this meeting was scheduled at the last moment."

"Actually I live and work in Valdosta now, but I was summoned here, so here I am."

Tyrone smiles without saying what he is really thinking. "Let's walk over to the conference room" he says, as he steps out and closes his door behind him.

"So how have you been?" Tyrone asks "life must be good, because you haven't aged a day."

"Hah, please, looks can be deceiving. These have been the roughest six months of my life. Spent my life focusing on my career, put off starting a family, and now… now I'll never be able to do that."

"Well, consider yourself blessed. I was almost executed, now they're trying to save my life, but not because they believe I'm innocent. I'm anxious to hear what they have to say today."

"I'm anxious to hear what they have to say too" Jennifer says.

After they arrive in the conference room they don't have to wait long. Soon Penny Wright arrives, followed by the Governor. The Governor's bodyguards wait outside as the door is closed, and she shakes everyone's hand and then sits down before saying. "Now that we've gotten through all the pleasantries, let's deal with the elephant in the room. Mr. Marshall, you are mankind's... or should I say, womankind's only hope. The babies that are born this year may not live as long as their parents because there will not be a younger generation to care for them. The human race could be less than a hundred years away from extinction. Having met with the President and the head of the CDC, I am willing to do my part in making the following proposal work. First of all let me apologize with respect to the first proposal. I had no knowledge of it and I would never have agreed with it. I think it was disrespectful and insensitive. You're not an animal, and you should not be treated as such. That being said, this new proposal addresses some very critical and important points which I would like you to take special note of. Every country on this planet will be sending one hundred and eighty women here to Atlanta. Over the next 12 months, their goal is to become pregnant by means of direct interaction with you. Once their pregnancy is confirmed, they will return to their home country. Currently there are 196 countries in the world if we include Palestine, so that's 35,280 pregnancies. Assuming at least one child per pregnancy, and half of them being girls, we can expect at least 17,640 boys being born per year. Now, the women being sent will be carefully selected. They will be from the most genetically desirable families, to minimize the possibility of birth defects and to guarantee that these future generations will be capable of learning all the skills required to keep society functioning. They will be the lawyers, engineers and professors of the future. You would only need to do this for eighteen years, until that first generation of boys become men and can take over the responsibility in their respective countries. By that time you would have fathered at least six hundred and thirty five thousand and forty children. You will more than likely not have enough time to study any profession in those eighteen years, but you will receive a monthly salary from the Federal Government. Not bad eh? If you accept the offer, I will grant you clemency on your conviction."

There is a deafening silence in the room as Tyrone looks up at the Governess and asks: "Do you think my life and my reputation can be bargained or negotiated away just like that? Come back when you decide to investigate how they railroaded me and almost took away my life."

With that, Tyrone gets up and walks out of the conference room and heads to his room. Thirty minutes later there is a knock on his door. Tyrone gets up and opens the door, it's Jennifer.

"Can I come in?"

"I'm a convicted rapist and murderer, are you sure that's a good idea?"

"Alleged murderer and rapist, besides, I'm your attorney, I think I'm safe."

Tyrone steps aside and Jennifer walks in before stopping in the middle of the room. He closes the door and sits down in the sofa before offering her a seat in the EZ chair.

"One of the things I regret not doing as a Public Defender was getting to know you. Truth is, I didn't want to be a Public Defender. My family life was not the best, Dad spent most of his time fishing or drinking and when he was at home he always seemed to be fighting with Mom. They were more drinking buddies than husband and wife. I took up softball because it kept me out of the house, and when I wasn't playing softball I was studying hard so I wouldn't end up like my parents. I got good grades, got a partial scholarship, started college courses in high school, got my license to practice law at 25… but I couldn't get a job with a decent law firm, because my last name wasn't Kennedy, Rollins or Turner, and my parents were not exactly model citizens… and that's putting it nicely. Not even the DA's office hired me, instead I was sent to the Public Defender's office where we helped poor defendants negotiate a lighter sentence. I tried to fight your case to make a name for myself but my boss said: "They all say they didn't do it". I didn't want to rock the boat or ruffle any feathers, so I did what my boss said and the first chance I got to land a decent job elsewhere I took it, with my former boss' glowing recommendation. I feel like a sellout."

After a few minutes of silence, Jennifer could hear Tyrone adjusting himself in the sofa, but she didn't dare look him in the face.

"I was my Mom's second child, my brother's dad was already married and my mom didn't know. He sent her money every month after he moved away with his family, but he never made any effort to come visit my brother. I guess my mom was desperate to have a man in the house, so she made the mistake of sleeping with another man again before she got married to him, and that's how I came about. My dad died of an accident on the job when I was only five years old, and my brother died in a gang shootout when I was only fifteen. When I was in High School, our girls' softball team played against another school and they had this very good pitcher. She was beautiful, about five feet nine inches tall, red hair, freckles on her face and big and strapping, just like me. All the boys were intimidated by her, but I liked her. She was older than me though, and I was just a black kid from a low income family. My goal was to study hard and become a Paramedic, then maybe one day I would run into her again... I did, she was my Public Defender."

Tyrone's voice trails off as he lowers his head and bursts into tears like a small child. Jennifer is shaking her head from side to side as she looks up with her mouth wide open. Soon she is overcome with emotion and she starts crying also. "Tyrone, I didn't know."

The two cry for what seems like an eternity, but it's only five minutes. Jennifer gets up from the EZ chair and sits beside Tyrone: "You're innocent, and I'm going to make it my job to clear your name."

"Why, because I told you a sad story?"

"No Tyrone, no. We've represented all kinds of people in court, and there is no criminal who would have refused the offer you got today just so that they could clear their name and reputation. Right now you hold all the chips, and yet your biggest concern is that you were railroaded and you want to set the record straight. That's the sign of an innocent man. I'm going to start working on this right away. Here's my card with my cell number, text me so that I can store your number." With that Jennifer leaves, and Tyrone stretches out in the sofa with his eyes closed as he inhales her lingering perfume.

Chapter 6 – A Compromise

"Hi Penny, it's Jennifer... yes I spoke to him. His mind is made up, I think we should go over the case together for maximum transparency. I kept personal copies of everything, and I have them with me, can we meet at your office tomorrow morning? Great, I'll see you at 10:00am, bye."

Jennifer heads to her hotel and after changing into something more comfortable she starts reviewing her file on Tyrone. Tyrone by this time has completed his daily workout and taken a shower. His mother is here for her visit, and the two talk and reminisce over dinner. After dinner they turn on the TV to watch the news, just in time to hear the following: "Thank you for joining us, a social media post claims that the District Attorney's office is reviewing the murder and rape conviction of Georgia death row inmate Tyrone Marshall. This has fueled wild speculation that Tyrone Marshall is the lone survivor of the outbreak that the President referred to in her speech not long ago. We reached out to the DA's office for comment, but so far they have not responded, and the social media post has since been deleted and the user account closed. In other news tonight, Ambassadors from all over the world have been flying in to New York today as the United Nations has called an emergency meeting that will not be open to the public or the press."

Tyrone and his mother look at each other in unison as his mother says "oh, lawd have mercy, I can't go home tonight!" So she spends the night with her son, but the next day they are up bright and early. They turn on the TV and every single channel is talking about the scheduled press conference with the Governor of Georgia at 10:00am. Tyrone turns off the TV right away and starts preparing breakfast as his mother nervously looks out the window. After breakfast they try to distract their minds, but as 10:00am approaches they turn on the TV as everyone awaits the Governor's press conference. As soon as the clock changes to 10:00am, the Governor approaches the podium.

"Good morning everyone. As a country, and as a worldwide family, we have been through a lot these past 6 months and I want to commend everyone for the brave way you have handled the adversity. As we recover from this adversity, we will have to endure **more** difficult times, new feelings, new emotions, new philosophies, some of them pleasant and some of them unpleasant. Let's rise to the occasion. From the despair of death and sadness, let's work together to chart our own destiny by embracing new ideas. By being humble enough to recognize our mistakes from the past and being willing to correct them. I would like to confirm that the lone survivor of the outbreak is indeed Georgia death row inmate Tyrone Marshall. For obvious reasons we could not reveal that information before, however, circumstances have changed. We believe that Mr. Marshall's life is no longer in danger from the outbreak and as the newly appointed governor, I, unlike my predecessor believe that executions should only occur if there is absolutely no shadow of doubt. At this point I have doubt, and for this reason I have asked the DA's office to review Mr. Marshall's conviction, with the assistance of the Public Defender's Office and Mr. Marshall's counsel at the time of his conviction. Now are there any questions?"

"Governor, there is a rumor going around that the government is looking for a loophole to release Mr. Marshall so that he can help repopulate the planet, wouldn't that be a perversion of justice?"

"That doesn't make sense. I'm the Governor, it is my prerogative to grant clemency to whomever I wish, so if that were really the case I would have simply granted him a pardon. No, this request came from Mr. Marshall himself, and his attorney can attest to that fact. We no longer live in a male dominated society, so we're not worried about bruised egos. Our concern here is truth and justice. Next question."

"Governess, is there any truth to the rumor that the emergency meeting at the UN is related to Mr. Marshall's case?"

"I have not been informed of that, you may want to direct that question to the State department, next question."

"Governess, how soon should we expect the findings on Mr. Marshall's case?"

"I didn't set a deadline, I am going to let the law take its natural course. However, since criminal proceedings are not sealed you should be able to see any developments by searching the court's website for updates. Next question?"

"Will Mr. Marshall be released pending the findings?"
"There is no legal basis to release Mr. Marshall at this point in time. He is still under the supervision of the Georgia Department of Corrections, although his place and manner of incarceration are a bit... let us say... unorthodox. Based on the findings, his attorney may choose to file a motion to have him released, and if and when that motion is filed, it will be addressed by the courts based on merit. That's all the questions I'll take for now, and I implore you to please respect the privacy of Mr. Marshall and his family."

With that the Governor leaves the podium as Tyrone turns off the TV and embraces his mother. It's the best news they have heard in years and they both shed tears of joy. Soon his mother is on her way and Tyrone is alone in his prison, but somehow he feels liberated.

The next day, the whole nation is abuzz with news that Jennifer has filed a motion for a retrial based on newly discovered evidence. With the male population wiped out and crime at an all-time low, the hearing is set for Friday of that same week. Tyrone already knew because Jennifer had called last night to let him know that she had filed the motion electronically. Tyrone in turn called his mother to give her the news.

The week flew by quickly, and on Friday morning Tyrone is taken by a Department of Corrections vehicle to the courthouse. He is not handcuffed, and is dressed in a nice twill suit with a dark grey base interwoven with tropical colors and a nice floral tie to match over a long white sleeve shirt. His mother got the expensive suit for free, but she had to make a few adjustments so that it would be a perfect fit.

As Tyrone walks into the Courthouse, he can see his mother seated a row behind the Defense table with Tyrone's cousin Desiree. Jennifer greets him with a hug and a smile, then invites him to sit, as Penny confers with her assistant over by the Prosecution table. The court is abuzz with excitement as the women whisper among themselves. The judge has allowed a single camera crew into the courtroom, with the condition that they share the live broadcast with other media outlets. Little does Tyrone realize that the entire world population is tuned in to the broadcast.

As the bailiff says "All rise…" the judge walks in and takes her seat, then everyone else is invited to retake their seats. "Good morning everyone. I have read the Defendant's motion, but before I make a ruling I would like to hear the Prosecution's stance on this matter."

Penny rises from her chair and looks at the judge. "Your honor, the Prosecution supports the Defense's position of the need for a retrial, however, the Prosecution does not believe this case has merit. It is no longer our position that Mr. Marshall committed this crime, and in fact, we urge the court to vacate his conviction and send him back to his family where he rightfully belongs."

"After reading the Defense's motion I would tend to agree, but what is troubling to me counsellor is that you were part of that prosecution. How did you end up sending an innocent man to death row for ten years?"

"Your honor, I was a young prosecutor sitting second chair on my first Capital Punishment case. I was learning from the lead prosecutor, and although I saw some anomalies, the lead prosecutor at the time told me that it was the Defense's job to raise those points if they had any merit. He asked me to trust the work of the detectives and being as young and naïve as I was, I took his word as gospel."

"Which brings me to the Defense" the judge says as she looks at Jennifer "didn't you see those anomalies?"

"I did your honor, and like my colleague I was a young attorney handling my first major case with the Public Defender's office. My boss at the time asked me to get a deal to take the death penalty off the table, and before I knew it we were at trial. My boss sat in as lead counsel and decided strategy, but I basically argued the case. So I had to argue a case based on my boss' strategy, which I wasn't in complete agreement with, but in a male dominated society it would have been career suicide to do otherwise. Besides, as a young attorney I didn't have the confidence or the experience to challenge my boss. What if I were wrong? I would have looked like a fool."

"I understand, and it's sad that things have reached this point. But humankind is on the brink of a new beginning, and I hope that we can use this opportunity to right many of the wrongs of the past and chart a much better course for the future. Mr. Marshall, the conviction against you has been vacated, you are a free man." There is spontaneous applause in the courtroom, but the judge allows it before she formally adjourns the court and returns to her chambers.

Tyrone is embraced by his mother and cousin and after hugging and crying for a few minutes they start the long walk out of the courtroom and to the vehicle. Tyrone had entered through the back earlier that morning so he was surprised as he exited the courtroom and saw the thousands gathered. There were cheers of delight and applause, but all of that stopped suddenly as Tyrone and his mother were rushed by a group of reporters.

"Tyrone, how does it feel to be a free man?"
"Liberating."
There is loud laughter as Tyrone's witty comment resonates with the women.
"Tyrone, what are your plans, now that you are free?"
"Well the first thing I'd like to do is to spend some quality time with my family and catch up on what I've missed out on these past ten years. And please guys, I know you all want a story, but please respect my privacy and the privacy of my family. I'm going to start a social media account and you can get all your updates there okay? Now let me take one last picture with my family and my attorney and that's it, here goes."

Tyrone poses on the steps of the courthouse as the reporters and photographers step back to get the picture. Jennifer stands to his left and his mother to his right, then Desiree beside his mother. They pose for about 30 seconds as the photographers take several pictures, then Jennifer says goodbye and heads to her vehicle, as Tyrone and his family head to Desiree's vehicle.

Chapter 7 – The Catch

When Tyrone arrived at his mother's house, he was shocked to see all the mail he had received. Most of it is from within Georgia. Tyrone's mother was a housekeeper and nurse for an older couple, but after the outbreak started the husband died quickly, and his widow decided to leave the house to Tyrone's mother in her Will. It's a nice house in a gated neighborhood, but there is no guard during the day, just between sunset and sunrise. During the day you have to use a code to open the gate.

Tyrone's mother had studied nursing after Tyrone went to prison, and she lived a simple life in her small rental apartment not far from her job. After her boss died she practically moved in with his widow so that she could attend to her around the clock, but she too died about two months after. They had two boys, but the daughters-in-law were too busy with their own grief to even care about material things. As the bodies piled up, Tyrone's mother was hired by the state to help document, take samples from and bury the dead men.

The house has three bedrooms, and Tyrone's mother has taken up residence in the guest room. It's obvious that she still has stuff in her apartment, as her room has mostly items of clothing. She leads Tyrone to the master bedroom which she has prepared for him and he immediately climbs into the bed. It's one of those electric beds, similar to a hospital bed that allows you to raise and lower both ends. This bed is queen sized though, allowing Tyrone's body to fit comfortably as he raises his head just enough to be able to watch the TV comfortably. Before he could turn on the TV though, Desiree starts to bring in the boxes of mail from the Post Office. All the envelopes have a yellow sticker, because they have been forwarded to this address from his mother's apartment.

As Tyrone begins to open the letters he realizes that most of them have pictures of the women. Most of the letters are from the same county where he grew up and a few others from neighboring counties. One letter in particular caught his eye, because the writer said she was confident he would be released, and she even asked him to friend her on Facebook once he is released.

Just then Tyrone leaps from the bed and walks over to an area which is like a small extension to the master bedroom. It's a little office area where the previous owners have a top of the line computer with a massive 32 inch monitor. Tyrone turns on the computer and it boots up very quickly. Typical of the elderly, who like to keep things simple, there is no password. The computer is running Windows 10, but the interface looks like Windows 7, which was what Tyrone last used before he went to prison. Tyrone has no problem using the computer, but before he can use Facebook he needs to reactivate his old Yahoo email address. Because he had not used it for such a long time there were no emails, but after signing up on Facebook, he got his first new email after ten years.

Right away Tyrone searched for the woman who sent him that letter with the Facebook invite and friended her. Tyrone had heard about Facebook, it was founded before he went to prison, but it was never something that he was interested in. Before he could walk away from the computer Zoe accepted his friend request, but Tyrone is anxious to read the other letters so he heads straight to the bed to continue reading. Most of the letters have modest pictures, but a few women send pictures of themselves in bikinis.

Tyrone is relieved to be outside the walls of the CDC, to finally be a free man. All the bitterness and resentment that he felt when they tried to bargain his freedom with him have disappeared, and he is now enjoying the reading of all the letters.

It's almost 12:00PM when Desiree informs Tyrone that lunch is almost ready, so he walks over to the computer and looks at his Facebook page. Tyrone is surprised to find that he has almost 5 million friend requests and over 10 million likes for his profile picture: That famous picture that he took on the court steps just this morning with Jennifer, Desiree and his mother. Tyrone clicks the option to accept "all" the friend requests, then he heads for the dining area. His mother is all smiles as she finishes up with the stove and heads to the table. She asks Tyrone to say grace and then they start to eat, southern style fried chicken, mashed potatoes, gravy, Cole slaw and corn on the cob, plus a glass of apple cider.
Tyrone dug into his food like a man who had not eaten in many days, then he slowed down the pace and started to smile with his mother and cousin.
"I now have five million friends on Facebook" Tyrone says.
"Five million?" Desiree shouts as her mouth hangs wide open.
"Yep".
"Wow Tyrone, that's a new record."
The family of three eat and talk about Tyrone's new found fame and his plans for the future, but he is not sure what he wants to do with his life yet. Right now he just wants to go back onto Facebook. For years he was cut off from America, now

the world has opened up to him. As soon as he is done eating he washes up and heads to the master bedroom. He has another 3 million friend requests and he accepts all of them. In addition, he has over 15 million followers. Tyrone spends a major portion of the afternoon on Facebook as he reads all the messages of encouragement, then Desiree walks in with another container from the Post Office with more mail. Tyrone thanks her then lays down in bed as he goes through the letters.

Except for a bathroom break, Tyrone doesn't leave the bed as he goes through every single letter. Desiree has left and it is almost sunset, his mother walks in with a slice of apple pie and some peach flavored hot tea and says: "Turn on the TV."
Tyrone turns on the TV just in time to catch the start of the news report.
"And at the top of our news report this evening, former Georgia death row inmate Tyrone Marshall opened up a Facebook account this morning. His first friend was Florida socialite Zoe Chandiram, the heiress to the Chandiram business empire. Zoe's brothers were being groomed to take over the Chandiram business empire, as she spends most of her time travelling the world on private jets and spending her father's money. Zoe has been the subject of many rumors in the past regarding drunk and disorderly conduct, but a few weeks ago the thirty five year old says that she has turned over a new leaf and is looking to be more responsible, now that her father and brothers have died."
The next newscaster says: "Well, I'm sure she would want to increase her chances of snatching the only eligible bachelor in the civilized world."
"Ooh" the first newscaster coos, "somebody is going to get fired."
They both laugh as the second newscaster continues: "Tyrone now has over five million friends on Facebook, and almost thirty million followers, wow!"
Tyrone and his mother look at each other as the newscasters continue.

"Also in the news tonight, all UN member nations have voted unanimously to ratify the **Humankind Regeneration and Conservation Treaty**. With this ratification, all member nations will now pass laws that will allow the treaty to work within the confines of each country's constitution."

As Tyrone's mother picks up the empty plate and heads to the kitchen, he slides out of bed and walks over to the computer. He is taking a closer look at Zoe's Facebook profile, which looks much different from how it used to be. He knows this because he has googled her and looked her up on Wikipedia and she was and probably still is a wild one. However, she seems to be working on cleaning up her image. Tyrone heads back to the bed and disconnects his cell phone from the charger, before dialing Jennifer's number.

"Good evening Miss O'Riley, are you busy?"

"Not really, I can talk. Did you see the news?

"Yes I did, and I'm sorry, I had no idea who she was."

"I'm not talking about that" Jennifer responds "that's the least of my concerns. I'm talking about the **Humankind Regeneration and Conservation Treaty.**"

"Oh yes, I saw that" Tyrone says.

"So what do you think?"

"I think it's a nice initiative to keep people financially safe while not creating an economic chaos."

"That's the first part Tyrone, what about the second part?"

"There's a second part?"

"Yes, there's a second part. In the second part, it says that anyone who uses genetic or biological material to try and destroy human life is guilty of a human rights violation and should face life in prison if found guilty. If they actually kill anyone in the process, the penalty is death…"

"Jennifer, in view of what we have been through that makes a lot of sense."

"True, but part 'b' of that says that anyone who withholds or refuses to share genetic or biological material that could save or extend human life is also guilty of the same crime."

"Oh darn, they're coming after me aren't they?"

"You got it buddy."

"Is that why my conviction was vacated?"

"No, you're case had enough merit for it to be vacated. However, it's not common for those cases to be decided so quickly. Truth be told, having the prosecutor support me really helped, but still, it was fast."

"So Jennifer, what do we do?"

"Wait… let's see what their next move is. In the meantime, be careful what you post on social media."

"Okay, will do, thanks for everything, I'll keep in touch, bye."

"Bye Tyrone."

Tyrone disconnects the call and rolls over in bed as he realizes the gravity of his situation.

Chapter 8 – First Blow

For a long time now Tyrone's mother had stopped being the dreamy, carefree girl. She had become a very practical and realistic woman, doing her best to raise her sons the right way. And although she couldn't save one, she did her best to save the second along with a little help from an unlikely source. She had saved in a trinket box, Tyrone's old driver's license, his birth certificate, some baby pictures and some other items of sentimental value. As a result, Tyrone was able to renew his driver's license. He bought a work van with ease, because his mother has excellent credit and was his co-signer, that and the fact that car dealerships are desperate to sell vehicles. Desiree showed him how to create a business page on Facebook, and within an hour of creating the page for handyman services, he had appointments scheduled for the rest of the month.

Tyrone works at a relaxed pace, and likes to start at 9:00 AM and finish his last job around 4:00 PM. After taking a shower and turning on the TV to watch the news, he became aware of the new Georgia law that aligns itself with the **Humankind Regeneration and Conservation Treaty.**

Just then the doorbell rang and Tyrone got up to answer the door. He opened the door to find a tall African American Sheriff's deputy standing at the door. "Tyrone Marshall, you have been served."

Tyrone accepts the envelope and closes the door, before going to his bedroom to read the information. The letter is from the State Health Department, ordering him to contact the department within seven days to arrange "genetic material sharing, for the conservation of society and human existence". The letter also highlights that if he fails to comply, he could be imprisoned for life.

Tyrone picks up his phone and calls Jennifer right away. Jennifer asks him to scan and send a copy to her via email.

"So what do we do?" Tyrone asks.

"I'm just your attorney" Jennifer says "tell me what you want to do and I'll do it."

"I don't want to jump into bed with any strange woman, much less thousands of women. When I lose my virginity, I want it to be with the woman I marry."

There was a moment of extended silence and then Jennifer says "okay, I'll draft a motion to challenge the constitutionality of the law."

"Sounds good, keep me posted."

"Will do Tyrone."

It takes just a few days for Tyrone to realize how difficult it is to work alone. He's afraid of being alone with certain women, so he asks his cousin if she would be willing to give up her job to work with him. Desiree would like to help her cousin, but she's gaining invaluable experience in the profession she studied at Community College. Unfortunately she has to refuse his offer.

Within a week Tyrone's hearing is scheduled, and he has to postpone all his appointments for that day in order to attend court. Penny Wright is representing the State, to Tyrone's surprise. After going through all the formalities Jennifer is invited to present her arguments.

"Your honor, as explained in my brief, this new law violates the 14th amendment of the United States Constitution which says in part in section one: "No State shall make or enforce any law which shall abridge the privileges or immunities of citizens of the United States". Forcing Mr. Marshall to have a sexual relationship with thousands of women is state sponsored rape, and is also a violation of his First Amendment rights. Mr. Marshall professes the Christian faith, wherein a sexual relationship outside the confines of marriage is considered fornication. A sin."

The judge acknowledges Penny and she proceeds with her argument. "Your honor, humankind has suffered a tragedy that the founding fathers and early lawmakers could never have imagined in their wildest dreams. Every single country on this planet has ratified the **Humankind Regeneration and Conservation Treaty.** A major event has taken place that has forced us as a society to redefine our norms. Mr. Marshall cannot use his religious or moral norms to hold the entire planet hostage."

"Your honor, Mr. Marshall is not holding the entire planet hostage. He didn't cause this crisis. Besides, Mr. Marshall is not the only male on this planet."

Penny responds quickly with frustration in her voice. "Your honor, counsel knows very well that the other men on this planet live in isolated tribes that are aggressive and violent. It would take us decades to communicate with them and build their trust to the point that we could work together on this matter."

"Then I would recommend that they get started as soon as possible" Jennifer responds, as the courtroom breaks out into laughter.

Penny flashes her a cold stare and then says: "Your honor, those individuals are neither US citizens, nor do they live within the jurisdiction of the United States. Besides, based on what we know about this bacteria, those men would become infected and later die once they make contact with a woman from outside their tribes."

"Isn't there a vaccine that you could give them?"

"No your honor, we have not been able to successfully develop a vaccine for women, and although we have a vaccine for men, it is so far untested because we have no test subject."

The judge takes a deep breath and looks around the courtroom. "Because this law is very general in its wording, I'm not willing to declare it unconstitutional, at least not yet. However, that being said I will make certain rulings that should not violate Mr. Marshall's constitutional guarantees. Miss O'Riley, you did mention in your brief that there is no evidence to conclusively prove that any male child born to Mr. Marshall would be protected by an acquired immunity from its father. I agree. So before we can address that issue, we need to be sure about the science. Miss O'Riley, your client has over 50 million followers on Facebook. I don't believe he should have a problem getting married within ninety days to someone who shares his religious and moral convictions. After getting married, he is ordered to try and have a child right away. Having children is a personal decision that normally the court doesn't get involved in. However, I believe that the scientific knowledge gained will result in benefits not only for humankind in general, but also for Mr. Marshall. When all is said and done, we still don't know everything about this bacteria; whether it will mutate etcetera. I'd like to see everyone back here in ninety days. My clerk will send both parties written copies of my decision, and the date for the next hearing. This case is adjourned."

After leaving court, Tyrone invites Jennifer to have lunch at his place, which she accepts. Tyrone quickly prepares a delicious salad and they both sit down to eat in the kitchen, seated around the counter. They talk for a bit about the case and the judge's decision, then there is silence. Tyrone stops chewing his salad and looks up because he realizes Jennifer isn't eating. Jennifer is staring at him and even when their eyes make four she doesn't look away. Her tough lawyer demeanor has melted away and she looks into his eyes as if she were looking for something specific. She finally realizes what she is doing and slowly turns away to look down at her plate. "Jennifer, what is it?"

As a tear rolls down Jennifer's face she says: "When I was talking to you the other day on the phone… I felt bad when you spoke about your virginity, because I simply assumed the opposite. I regret not working hard enough to keep you out of prison."

"You did your best Jennifer… given the circumstances. This tragedy has forced humankind to take a fresh look at the way we do things. It's not your fault, like me you were a victim of the society you lived in."

A tear rolls out of Jennifer's other eye and Tyrone pushes his plate away and slowly spins her stool around to face him. She still doesn't look up so he stretches out his hand to hold hers, but instead of giving him her hand she stands up quickly and embraces him. Tyrone closes his eyes as her body presses against his. Her long orange colored hair is alive with the sweet aroma of some exotic shampoo, and he can feel the temperature rising quickly between their bodies.

"Jennifer, will you marry me?"

He can hear her gasp with surprise as her body begins to shake. Releasing her embrace, she pushes back a bit to look him in the eyes and Tyrone becomes lost in time as he stares into her big bluish green eyes. Her mouth quivers and more tears flow as she tries to speak, but the words don't come out, so she shakes her head in the affirmative and hugs him again. When she calms down a bit she finally says: "yes".

Atlanta traffic is not what it used to be, within minutes they are at the courthouse getting their marriage license. Now, with their license in hand they are declared man and wife by a magistrate and after completing the paperwork they head back home. Jennifer drives while Tyrone sends pictures to his mother and Desiree.

"Don't you dare post anything on Facebook… at least not yet." Jennifer says, with a huge smile on her face.

"Naah, I'm just sending the pictures to Mom and Desiree."

Later on that evening, as Tyrone's mother enters the house, the place is dead quiet. On the master bedroom door there is a beautiful sign that says: "Just married". Apparently Tyrone made it on the computer. She decides not to disturb them and instead goes to the kitchen to unpack the stuff she bought. As she puts away the last few items, Tyrone emerges and embraces his mother who begins to weep tears of joy. Soon Jennifer emerges wearing one of Tyrone's cotton sweat suits. Her nice figure fills out the sweat suit very well, and Tyrone's mother runs over to Jennifer quickly to give her a hug also.

The world economy has changed a lot, food is cheap because farmers have lowered prices to keep merchandise moving, and with roughly half of the planet's population gone, demand is much lower. The **Humankind Regeneration and Conservation Treaty** has allowed the creation of laws that allow the States and different countries all over the world to renegotiate insurance policies so that insurance companies do not collapse because of the massive payouts. Most of the insurance payouts have been waived in exchange for abandoned houses in nice communities and a guaranteed pension and free government healthcare. Laws are being put into place to prevent ghettos and depressed communities, but there is still a lot left to be legislated and debated before the changes can actually happen.

With many women working to keep the utilities and other things running, university courses are now giving credit for on-the-job experience. Crime is at an all-time low worldwide as many women are just too busy trying to help re-stabilize human society. The prisons still have female prisoners, but now, the few cases of arrest and trial have to do with theft and drug abuse. The demand for drugs has literally dried up, because women have pulled together like a large support group with a new purpose in life.

Tonight, Tyrone and Jennifer lie in bed reflecting. Reflecting on what has happened over the past ten years and trying to imagine the future. At almost thirty five years old, Jennifer considers herself very fortunate to be the one chosen by Tyrone to bear his children, and who knows, maybe even restart the human race.

The next day Tyrone posts a picture and a message to announce his marriage to the world. Many women are happy, but some are sad, others even mad. Tyrone works the next day, and Jennifer works remotely, but after he gets home they are visited by three FBI agents.

The FBI agents are very clear. In the interest of national security and public safety, Tyrone can no longer work, and neither can Jennifer. They are limited to staying within the community, and they must avoiding travelling outside the community without notifying the FBI. Their shopping has to be done by someone else, and if purchasing online they have to use someone else's name and credit card. Family members need to be pre-approved by the FBI before they can come and visit, or learn where they live. They can monitor their Facebook page and like comments, but they can't post any new material without approval from the Department of Homeland Security. In addition, they will both receive a monthly salary from the federal government.

As the agents leave, Tyrone and Jennifer look at each other as they realize just how much their lives will continue to change. As they withdraw to their bedroom for the evening, they turn on the TV to watch the news. All male babies that have been born since the outbreak are dying within a week of being born, and the mothers are distraught.

Television programming and scheduling has changed greatly. Sports is basically nonexistent right now, as the entire world population is caught up with stabilizing the social and economic chaos caused by the deaths of the men. The number of new videos posted on YouTube daily has dropped to almost zero, and older do-it-yourself videos have seen an increase in the number of views. All over the world, older movies and TV shows depicting a stable family life with a loving and exemplary father have taken over the programming. As they skip through the channels they come to a talk show, and Tyrone's Facebook page is on a TV screen in the background.

The hostess is interviewing a sociologist who says: "I am very happy for Mr. Marshall and his marriage to Jennifer, I think they make a wonderful couple. However, he needs to be a bit more balanced. I don't think a loving god would be okay with him denying humankind the opportunity to regenerate and save itself." Just then the host says: "But now that he's married, it's a whole new ballgame isn't it? Adultery is illegal many countries and is a basis for divorce here in the United States."

"That is correct" the sociologist replies "and that is why today, all fifty states passed the 'Marshall Exemption' marriage act. In fact, in states like Georgia where the governor was present for the passing of the bill, it was signed into law with immediate effect."

Tyrone and Jennifer turn to look at each other, they had no idea that such a bill was even passed, or the fact that it became law. As they turn around to look back at the TV, the hostess says: "So explain to us please what the 'Marshall Exemption' is?" "So basically, as you rightly said, a married man would be considered adulterous if he had a sexual partner other than his wife. The 'Marshall Exemption' would allow a man to have one wife but father many children with other women. In addition, those children would not legally be his responsibility, and they would bear the last name of the mother, or of her late husband."

"But isn't that a recipe for disaster as far as inheritance etcetera? In the past we have had problems with households where there was no father figure. How do we deal with a world where there is only one man and tens of thousands of baby boys being born each year?"

"That is a concern, and there were safeguards put in place to address those concerns. First off all, in ancient Israel, there was something known as brother in-law marriage. The way that worked was, if a married man died without leaving any children. His brother was allowed to have children with his widow, however, the children would not be considered children of the living brother. From an inheritance and legal point of view, they would preserve all the rights and privileges of the dead husband. Now the purpose of that law was to guarantee that the inheritance did not leave the family. It fulfilled the woman's natural desire to have children, and it also guaranteed that she had someone to care for her in old age. Brother in-law marriage was part of the law the prophet Moses received from God. Now as you know, three major branches of religion consider Moses a prophet, as well as other smaller religious groups. In addition, polygamy is widely accepted or tolerated in Africa and many Muslim countries. So we don't see a major problem here. In fact, the 'Marshall Exemption' expires six months after the first child produced by the 'Marshall Exemption' turns eighteen. At that time each country will be free to revise its laws to take into consideration the increase in the male population".

"Well that sounds very reasonable" the host says.

"Yes it is" the sociologist replies, "in fact, one of the things that will be done is that children will be taught in history class how the human race almost died out, and the role Mr. Marshall played in saving humanity. Mr. Marshall will become a folk hero, not just a national hero, but rather an international hero. And let me add real quickly that a lot of the things that we used to watch on TV were socially destructive, especially to the family. You probably realized that the programming on TV these days has changed?"

"Yes I have, and I would say for the better."

"Well that's something we as sociologists recommended. In a world without men, both the girls living now and the children that will be born will need to learn what it means to be a true man as well as what should be expected from a true man. We have carefully selected shows and movies from the 1950s to the 1990s that reflect a stable family environment, and those are the examples that we will be showing our children. By the time they become adults, they will have a good understanding of what is expected from them."

"So basically we have a very bright future ahead of us?" The TV host asked.

"Yes, BUT! And there's a big BUT here. It all depends on one person." This she says as she looks right into the camera. Tyrone knows that her last comment is directed towards him, so he turns off the TV in disgust. Jennifer rolls over and gives him a hug while sighing deeply.

"That interview was all staged" Tyrone says "they want to influence public opinion and put us under pressure."

"I know" Jennifer replies.

"What do we do?" Tyrone asks.

"Wait... that's all we can do. We have court in a little under ninety days. The fact that we got married and are trying to get pregnant right away is a sign that we are willing to be reasonable. What we need to do right now is anticipate what their arguments will be and prepare ourselves thoroughly. We can't make any public comments like on Facebook or YouTube that would show our hand. Let's catch them by surprise."

"I know there was a reason I married you" Tyrone says "you're so smart."
"If I were smart you wouldn't have gone to prison in the first place."
"Are we still talking about that? Baby, please, let it go, I don't hold you responsible for that."
There was a long silence, and suddenly Tyrone became very sad and insecure. Looking straight up into the dark ceiling he asked: "Did you get married to me out of pity? Do you really love me, or am I just a free ticket to your future?"
"Tyrone, how could you say that?" Jennifer asks in a loud voice.
The words were barely off her lips when Jennifer started to cry and immediately there was a knock on the bedroom door.
"Sorry to barge in" Tyrone's mother says "but this is the first and last time I'll be doing this. Congrats! You've had your first fight."

Tyrone's mother ambles through the dark room, lit up only by the soft glow of the LEDs on the surge protector, and the smoke detector mounted in the ceiling. Jennifer is dressed in a night gown, but she pulls the sheet up to her neck anyway as she tries to suppress the tears. Tyrone's mother sits in the chair over by the computer. They can't see her face, but they know she is looking in their direction.

"Tyrone never told me about you, but I knew he liked you when he was in High School." Tyrone's heart races as his mother's words fall on his ears. He doesn't ask the question, because he knows his mother is going to answer anyway. "He only travelled to his school's away games when they played your school. His uncle gave him a camera as a gift, and you were the only player in all the pictures. Tyrone was so focused on studying, and even though all his friends had girlfriends, he didn't, because he was too busy working and studying. There's only one thing that can make a man focused and motivated like that... love. Jennifer, I can see you're a no-nonsense woman who would intimidate most men. Tyrone is physically big, just like you, and he is smart and witty. He's not intimidated by you, but he respects you. That's why you both fell in love. Tonight you both get a free pass, but let it be the last time you hurt each other with words. Let it be the last time you say unkind words to each other. If your words are not going to build up, don't say them. You kids have a lot of challenges ahead, you are going to need each other, save your energy for fighting side by side, not against each other."

With that Tyrone's mother rises from the chair and heads out of the room. The couple say nothing to each other, but they hold hands and cuddle up under the sheet before they eventually fall asleep.

Chapter 8 - Blitzkrieg

The next day, Tyrone is awakened to the sound of his mother leaving the house. He looks over at Jennifer who is still sleeping and then gently slides out of the bed, before heading over to the computer. The small extension to the master bedroom, where the computer is kept, cannot be seen from the bed. Tyrone gently rolls back the chair that his mother had pulled out the night before, then he touches the spacebar on the keyboard to wake up the computer, after which he turns on the large 32 inch screen. The Sun is just about rising, so Tyrone hopes the soft glow of the computer screen will be eclipsed by the superior glow of the rising Sun.

There are more than ten million notifications on his Facebook page, and Tyrone feels overwhelmed. Nevertheless, he clicks the notification of the mention of his name by the local TV station. The local TV station has a link to the video of the interview with the sociologist along with the following headline: "Sociologist says Tyrone Marshall is being 'unreasonable' for not wanting to help save the human family". After reading the article, Tyrone is livid. Right away he begins to type out a response, venting all his anger and frustration. As he begins to review the comment a voice behind him says: "Don't even think of posting that."

Tyrone is shaken with fright as he swivels the chair around to see Jennifer standing behind him. "Jennifer, you know what they're doing, I have to defend myself."

"True, but that's not the way to do it. Legally and morally they have a weak case, so they are trying you in the court of public opinion. They are contaminating possible jurors and trying to influence judges with public outrage. Don't say anything, at least not yet. Let everyone vent their anger and voice their opinion."

Tyrone looks up at Jennifer, she is not a petite woman. She is big, but she has a nice shape and her skin is flawless. The way her hair falls down the side of her head and down her chest is a beautiful thing to look at. And her bluish green eyes form such a nice contrast with her red hair and white skin which has an orange tinge. She walks up to Tyrone and stops an inch from his face. Tyrone directs his voice to her womb and says: "Is anyone in there?"

Jennifer laughs out loud then says "I think it's a bit too early for that."

"Okay, I'll try again next week" Tyrone replies.

"But first you need to delete that message" Jennifer says.

Tyrone reluctantly deletes the message and embraces Jennifer as they head back to bed.

An hour later they are out of bed again and heading to the kitchen for breakfast. After breakfast they decide to go for a walk in the neighborhood, which has a lot of trees. As they exit their driveway and head right, Tyrone realizes right away that they are being followed by a golf cart in the distance. Some of the neighbors are at home and they all smile at the couple as they make their way down the street. An older lady is tending to her garden near her fence, so Jennifer stops and greets her. They exchange pleasantries before Jennifer inquires as to why hardly anybody has been to their house or why people tend to go inside their houses as soon as they see the couple walking by.

"Well, you didn't hear this from me, but the FBI sent us a letter saying that we are forbidden from sharing the knowledge that you guys live here. Some people have gone to the extreme of shunning you guys all together, but not me. By the way, congrats on the wedding, I wish you guys all the best. My name is Martha by the way."

"Oh thank you Martha, nice to meet you" Jennifer responds.

"Nice to meet you too" Tyrone says.

As the two continue walking, they discreetly look back and notice the golf cart is still following them. They walk around the entire block holding hands and soon they are back home. As soon as they are inside they push a small part of the curtain aside. The golf cart is driven by two women who are with the security company that protects the neighborhood. The cart drives away and Tyrone and Jennifer head to the kitchen. Soon after there is a knock on the door. Tyrone looks through the peep hole and sees a well-dressed woman wearing an FBI badge.

Opening the door Tyrone says: "Good morning, how can I help you?"

"Tyrone Marshall, you have been served".

With that she turns and walks away before stepping into a black SUV and driving away. Jennifer walks up to Tyrone and takes the document from his hand.

"It's a Federal summons, let me take a look".

Jennifer opens the document and carefully goes over the pages while she slowly walks over to the sofa and sits down.

"According to this, the Federal Government alleges that the State of Georgia didn't have standing to handle matters regarding use of your genetic material. The judge ruled in their favor and we are now required to appear in Federal court in a two weeks for arguments."

"So you mean we have to go through this all over again?" Tyrone asks.

"Yes dear, we have to do this all over again, but I have a surprise for them."

Tyrone smiles as he cuddles his wife, he is so in love with his red haired attorney wife.

For the next three weeks, Tyrone and Jennifer prepare their case. Their first check from the Federal Government arrives, but they don't cash it. Jennifer is preparing a challenge to the government's position that they stay at home at all times out of a concern for national security. She is also challenging the government's position that Tyrone father children with other women as a public safety and health issue. The day before their court appearance, Jennifer calls Tyrone over to the computer and says: "Read this".

Tyrone begins to read the Facebook post which Jennifer has written as if she were Tyrone.

"Hi everyone. I'm sorry it took me so long to respond, but with several million posts appearing every day, it's kind of hard to figure out where to start. Anyway, it's impossible for me to read all the posts. If I were to dedicate 1 second to each post and I dedicated 12 hours per day to reading posts, I would only get through 43,200 per day. And of course that still wouldn't be practical. I have to dedicate time to family, especially now that my wife is expecting a baby."

Tyrone's eyes and mouth open wide as he turns to look at Jennifer who is all smiles. "Oh baby that's good news, I'm so happy, let's celebrate."

"Wait, finish reading what I wrote, I haven't actually posted it yet."

Tyrone continues: ""A Federal court has ruled that the State of Georgia does not have standing on this case, so we will be appearing before a Federal Judge tomorrow for a preliminary hearing. We hope that the judge respects our first and fourteenth amendment guarantees and rules against the government. Thanks to all who support us. Tyrone." Oh baby this is good, can I post this now?"

"Sure, go ahead."

Tyrone gets emotional as he looks at his beautiful wife: "Jennifer, I love you, I really do. Thank you for loving me for me. I'm going to do my best to be the best husband ever."

"Oh Tyrone" Jennifer says, as her voice breaks. They both embrace each other and shed a tear as the number of 'likes' and 'congratulations' jump from a few thousand to a few hundred thousand on Facebook.

The couple spend the rest of the day relaxing and watching old movies as well as prepare for court.

Chapter 9 – Square One

Jennifer and Tyrone are seated in the court wondering who the government's attorney will be. Two attorneys walk in and seat themselves behind the Plaintiff's table, but Jennifer only recognizes one of them. She is Genevieve MacTaggart, an experienced US attorney. Soon everyone rises to their feet on the bailiff's command as the judge walks in. After the formalities Miss McTaggart presents her argument.

"Honorable judge, this case is simple. Society's norms have been known to change over time, and those changes are usually for the benefit... the greater good so to speak of human society. With the existence of the human race in jeopardy, it is important that you find in favor of the government, thank you."

Now it's Jennifer's turn.

"This case is not about saving human society, it's about our Constitution. It's about respecting the rights of the individual in matters related to his religious beliefs, his conscience and his body. When our northern neighbors Canada realized that they had an aging population, they didn't force Canadian citizens to have more children, they made immigration easier, especially for families with more than two children. A few years ago we were belittling Mexicans and other Central Americans and blaming them for crime and everything that is bad. We wanted to deport all of them who were living in this country without a legal status. These are the same people who work long hours in fields, picking fruit and doing other menial tasks that Americans don't want to do. We spend millions on pet food and pet care every year, yet we couldn't find it in our hearts to pass reasonable immigration laws that would allow these people to come here on a temporary program to do farm work and then go back home. Instead we continued to allow coyotes to smuggle people in and have them work under some of the worst conditions with no benefits. Cheap labor, in exchange for low food prices. Since when did we care about the well-being of humankind? Right, when the 1% realized that in 80 years they could die and not be able to leave their millions to their kids or grandkids. The motive behind this action is selfish, and the court should not sanction institutionalized rape."

The judge scowls at the last remark and Jennifer knows right away that she has an uphill battle ahead of her.

"Having heard the preliminary arguments I do not feel that now is the time to make a decision regarding the Defendant's motion to dismiss" the judge replies. "I need to hear more on this matter that has no legal or historical precedent. Let's move ahead with trial starting tomorrow at 9:00am, court is adjourned."

Since the court allowed media cameras in the court room, the whole world is commenting on the case now, and almost every single TV channel has a panel of experts debating the issue. Tyrone arrives home with Jennifer and they both head to the bedroom. As Jennifer puts her briefcase away and slips into some more comfortable clothing, Tyrone gets onto the computer to see what's happening on Facebook. There are too many notifications for Tyrone to read them all, but one particular post grabs his attention. Someone has launched an online poll to find out from women worldwide if they believe Tyrone should father children with many women from different countries. Seventy percent are in favor, and thirty are against.

"Baby look at this!" Tyrone says. Jennifer walks over and says: "Take a screenshot of that, and print a copy also".

The other message that grabs Tyrone's attention is a video from Zoe Chandiram sent as a personal message. Tyrone clicks the 'play' button as he turns up the volume.

"Hi Jennifer and Tyrone, this is Zoe Chandiram, your very first Facebook fan and follower. Congrats on the baby, I hope it's a boy. Let me reassure you guys that you have my support one hundred percent. Wish you all the best, and by the way Jennifer, you did an excellent job today, bye."

The short video ends and Jennifer says: "Hmm, interesting" before she heads to the kitchen right away to satisfy her ravenous hunger. Tyrone clicks on Zoe's name and it takes him to her Facebook profile. Zoe has updated her profile again. She now lists her faith as "Christian". Tyrone mutes the volume and watches the video again. She is modestly dressed in a light blue dress that covers her bust almost to her neck, she seems to be wearing very light makeup, and there is a huge 'Holy Bible' on the shelf behind her. Her most recent post has pictures of her at the beach at sunrise, dressed in a white dress that reaches almost to her ankles, and the caption says: "Enjoying God's creation. The old Zoe never stopped to smell the roses or contemplate God's wonderful creation. The new Zoe confides in him and seeks his guidance everyday". Tyrone smiles as he clicks back to his Facebook profile. He couldn't help but realize how beautiful Zoe is. According to her Wikipedia profile, her father was from India and her mother a mix of Afro and Indian Trinidadian. She seems to have taken the best of both races as she is absolutely gorgeous, and her more humble demeanor is making her look even more attractive.

The next day, Tyrone and Jennifer are in court early. Media outlets from all over the world have set up, or are feeding off the video from the local channels. Soon it's nine o'clock and the judge walks in and takes a seat before everyone else sits down.
The prosecution is invited to present the opening argument, and Genevieve stands to address the judge: "Your honor, this case is not about the Constitution, it is about something much bigger, the survival of the human race. Mr. Marshall was wrongly incarcerated for ten years, and he is obviously bitter. However, that is no reason to hold the human race hostage. We will provide evidence to show that Mr. Marshall's position is selfish and that his desire is to write the future by making sure that all future generations will descend from his family only. Thank you."

Genevieve sits and the judge says: "The defense may now proceed with their opening arguments."
Jennifer rises and looks around the court before looking at the judge. "Your honor, this case has everything to do with the Constitution. My colleague has attempted to raise a smokescreen to distract us from the primary issues here. Nevertheless, we will show clearly that the prosecution's accusation of selfishness would be best directed at those who drafted this unconstitutional law. Thank you."

"The prosecution may call its first witness".
"Thank you your honor, the prosecution would like to call Miss Mary Caldwell to the stand."
Tyrone recognizes Miss Caldwell as the sociologist who appeared on TV to promote the '**Marshall Exemption**' law.

"For the record, please state your name and occupation."

"My name is Mary Caldwell, and I'm a lecturer of Psychology, Psychiatry and Sociology. I have Masters Degrees in all three disciplines, plus a PhD in Sociology."

"Thank you Miss Caldwell, now in your professional opinion, do you believe that the Federal Law that obligates Mr. Marshall to save the human race is unconstitutional?"

"No I do not."

"And why do you say so?"

"The framers of the Constitution could never have imagined in their wildest dreams that humankind would be in this predicament today. The purpose of the Constitution was to guarantee a stable and fair society, much different from the monarchies that their ancestors had fled in Europe. Thanks to that Constitution, the United States is recognized as a bastion of freedom and the place where many people want to live."

"Thank you, but the defendant has argued that the Federal version of the **Marshall Exemption** is a violation of his First and Fourteenth Amendment rights under the Constitution."

"Yes, Mr. Marshall did make that claim, however, Mr. Marshall claims adherence to the Christian faith which considers the Bible as their holy book. There is precedence in the Bible that would allow Mr. Marshall to accept and cooperate with the provisions of the **Marshall Exemption**."

"Are you referring to brother in-law marriage?"

"That is correct, I am referring to brother in-law marriage, and I don't think I need to go into any detail because it's a subject that has received a lot of media coverage."

"So, speaking purely as an experienced Psychiatrist, why do you think Mr. Marshall would not want to cooperate and help save the human family?"

"Objection your honor" Jennifer says, "calls for speculation."

"Your honor", Genevieve responds, "Miss Caldwell is an experienced health care and public health consultant. She is also licensed to practice in several states, she is more than qualified to give a professional evaluation based on the facts!"

"Overruled" the judge responds, "witness may answer".

"Mr. Marshall was wrongly convicted of a crime and sentenced to death. He lost all his appeals and should have been executed in January of this year. However, because of the outbreak, we delayed execution until we could figure out why he was not affected by the bacteria. During that time the District Attorney revisited his case and decided that the evidence did not support his arrest and conviction, and so his conviction was vacated. When a person like Mr. Marshall has suffered an injustice and eventually gains the upper hand, there is a rush of neural activity in the caudate nucleus of the brain. This is the part of the brain known to process rewards. It's what we call the psychology of retribution, or to put it in plain language, revenge. However, there is something that we call in psychology, the 'revenge paradox'. Basically the 'revenge paradox' is that terrible feeling that comes about when we carry out the revenge, but we end up not feeling as happy as we thought we would feel. As the only eligible man in the civilized world, Mr. Marshall is basking in the sweet revenge of being able to call the shots against the system that sent him to prison, and a world that has for the most part mistreated black people. In fact, he might even be entertaining the idea of watching the world population die out as he repopulates the world with his own children. However, he needs to bear in mind that he might be immune to the bacteria that wiped out the rest of the men, but he is not immune to the 'revenge paradox', and he will more than likely later regret his decision not to help save humankind from extinction."

"Thank you very much Dr. Caldwell. Your witness."
Jennifer accepts the invitation and approaches the witness box.
"Dr. Caldwell, apart from lecturing at the university do you have any other employers?"
"Well, like I mentioned before I serve as a consultant for several states and also the Federal Government."
"In fact Dr. Caldwell, would it be fair to say that you are one of the chief policy makers for the Federal Government?"
"I'm not a policy maker, but I am consulted by policy makers."
"Well they seem to implement your recommendations a lot, even though your recommendations often conflict with other experts in the field, isn't that so?"
"I don't keep track of how many of my recommendations are implemented as opposed to those of my colleagues who share a different opinion, so I really wouldn't know how to answer that question."

"Okay Dr. Caldwell, let's move on. You have said several times under oath that Mr. Marshall is refusing to "save" humankind. Isn't it true that Mr. Marshall and I are expecting a baby?"
"That is my understanding, yes."
"In fact, it is our intention to have several babies, wouldn't that help to keep the human family alive?"

"Well, assuming that you have a child every year until you reach menopause, and assuming that all of them are boys, that's only 15 boys. At 50 years old you would have your last child, and having 15 children would take a serious toll on your body. It's just not practical, you wouldn't have time for anything else."

"With no other women getting pregnant, I would have a lot of help wouldn't I?"

"I guess so, but leaving the future of the human population in the hands of one woman is a very slow process. Either you or your husband could die of another disease or an accident and that would put the population in jeopardy. When the girls who are born this year reach retirement age, there will not be enough people around to care for them. No doctors, nurses, farmers, firefighters, the list goes on and on."

"So basically you're saying that Mr. Marshall should violate his conscience and his religious beliefs to satisfy the future needs of humankind?"

"We believe that is a reasonable request, and as mentioned in my previous testimony, there is precedent in the Bible."

"But doesn't the Constitution prohibit the government from passing any laws regarding religion or the practice of religion?"

"The law doesn't mention religion, nor is it forcing Mr. Marshall to practice any specific religion. Mr. Marshall claims to adhere to the Christian faith and he claims that he is being reasonable. However, by pointing out his failure to adhere to a practice found in his own religious book, we are demonstrating that he is not being reasonable."

"Dr. Caldwell, are you a Christian?"

"No, I'm actually an atheist."

"So basically, you are trying to get Mr. Marshall to practice something you don't accept yourself, correct?"

"That is correct, and it may seem like a contradiction, but it isn't, it's his faith, it's his belief. He cannot choose to not follow his own faith on a whim, just to hold the rest of humankind as hostage."

"Dr. Caldwell, is it possible that your limited knowledge of Mr. Marshall's faith is affecting your interpretation of his actions?"

"I don't think so, the Bible is quite clear, I did actually read it". There is a light chuckle in the courtroom after Dr. Caldwell's comment.

"Dr. Caldwell, were you aware that the law regarding brother in-law marriage was given to Moses as part of the Mosaic Law, and was abolished with the establishment of Christianity?"

"I was not aware of that?"

"Obviously."

"Objection your honor" Genevieve says "counsel is testifying."

"Counsel will refrain from making such remarks and limit herself to asking questions", the judge says.

"Yes your honor, my apologies" Jennifer replies.

As the courtroom regains its composure from another round of chuckling, Jennifer continues with her questioning.

"So as an atheist you believe in Evolution?"

"Yes I do".

"And you accept the teachings of Charles Darwin?"

"Yes I do."

"So would you say we are witnessing natural selection right now?"

"We don't know how the bacteria came about, so it's hard to say."

"Are you saying it could have been a biological weapon?"

There is a loud gasp in the courtroom as everyone begins to look around at each other in fear.

"I'm not saying that."

"But you can't dismiss it either correct?"

"Not with the information we currently have, we simply don't have enough information to draw any firm conclusions."

"So assuming that Mr. Marshall were to get thousands of women pregnant, what guarantee do we have that those children would be born with no problems, or even survive the first two weeks?"

"We don't have any guarantees, but there are many women who are willing to take the risk, yourself included."

"But in my case, if my child is born retarded or with some defect, we will be able to take care of him or her. If the same thing happens to tens of thousands of women, wouldn't that create another crisis?"

"It probably would, but like I said, many women are willing to take that risk for the sake of humankind".

"Dr. Caldwell, how do you propose dealing with the issue of sexually transmitted diseases or genetic defects in prospective mothers?"

"We thought about that, and we have modified our posture a bit. All women who would bear children for Mr. Marshall would be of the Christian faith, they would be virgins, and would undergo extensive medicals."

"So basically, what you're saying is that under your plan, in another one hundred years, most if not everyone on the planet would be of the Christian faith?"
"That is a possibility."
"And as an atheist you are okay with that?"
"This is not personal, I'm simply doing my part to make sure that the human race survives."
"Miss Caldwell, human beings have done so much to ruin this earth. In the last twenty years we have had a rapid social decline. There has been a sharp increase in autism, cancer, global warming, and so many things. What if nature is simply pressing the reset button to save itself, what if it is God's will that we get off to a fresh start?"
"All of that is just pure speculation."
"True, it is speculation, but why do you and policy makers get to decide the destiny of the planet while violating someone's control over their own body? Isn't this why we have the 1st and 14th Amendments to the Constitution? No human being can say for sure what is happening and why, it's all speculation, and the Constitution is there to protect the common person from anyone who wants to self-perpetuate at the moral expense of others. Isn't that so?"
"I can't say I agree with everything you have said. I believe in the Constitution and all that it stands for, but I think as intelligent creatures we can adapt and make exceptions as needed. This is an extreme situation, a crisis, and even if there are areas of the Constitution that could be applied in a very narrow interpretation. I think the urgency of the situation requires that we all mutually agree to make an exception, for a specific period of time, until the danger no longer exists."
"I have no more questions for this witness your honor" Jennifer says.
"The witness is free to step down" says the judge.
Genevieve steps down from the witness box and heads to a seat in the first row behind the Prosecution.

"At this point the Prosecution would like to call Miss Marlene Samuels."
Marlene takes her position in the witness box and is sworn in.
"Please state your name and occupation for the record."
"My name is Doctor Marlene Samuels and I'm the head of the Center for Disease Control."

"Thank you Doctor Samuels. Now Doctor, could you explain to the court please why all our men have died, and the important role that Mr. Marshall can play in saving humanity?"

"Ok, well as you've all heard through the media. We have identified a bacteria that is responsible for killing all our men and boys. We still don't know why it only attacks males, and for some reason or the other Mr. Marshall was the only male whose body was able to trigger an immune reaction. So far we have been able to develop a vaccine using Mr. Marshall's blood, but it doesn't work on women. So women continue to carry the disease, and in fact many have passed it on to their newborn babies who have died after exposure. We believe that the vaccine would work on a child or a grown man, but a newborn baby's immune system is simply not developed enough to deal with this bacteria. We have every reason to believe that Mr. Marshall would pass on immunity to his unborn children, whose bodies would be ready to deal with this bacteria."

"Thank you Doctor Samuels. Now, how would the Marshal Exemption help humankind?"

"Well right now, if we didn't have Mr. Marshall to rest our hopes on, humankind would die off when all the girls born this year and those about to be born eventually die off. If Mr. Marshall just has kids with his wife, then over another sixty years, assuming they have about seven boys, Earth's population would dwindle to about 343 males and their wives, and any daughters they might have. Mr. Marshall would be ninety years old if he's still alive, all girls born this year would be sixty years old, and no longer capable of having children. Of course, if he and his sons and grandsons end up having more boys, then that figure would increase, but not by a whole lot. From that figure we would have to find doctors, nurses, farmers, etcetera to care for an aging population."

"So what is the benefit of Mr. Marshall having multiple children with women from all over the world?"

"There are many benefits. With a larger number of newborns, all the roles and occupations that I mentioned before would be filled. The elderly would have a younger generation to look after them, and with a larger genetic melting pot, it's less likely that a single disease could wipe out mankind. Mr. Marshall would be having children with the brightest, healthiest and most beautiful women on the planet. The lessons learned now will be used, and in fact are currently being used to pave the way for a better society. It's a win-win situation for both Mr. Marshall and humankind in general."

"Thank you Doctor Samuels. I have no more questions your honor, the prosecution rests."

Turning to Jennifer the judge says "would the defense like to cross?"

"Yes your honor. Miss Samuels, would it be fair to say that as the head of the CDC you have been at the forefront of the investigation into this strange bacteria?"

"That is correct, I work very long days, waking up as early as five in the morning and going to bed close to midnight."

"So, as the person who is at the forefront of the investigation, can you explain to us what has happened to the women who became pregnant before their men started dying?"

"All the women who were carrying male fetuses lost their babies to the bacteria within two weeks of birth."

"Why was that?"

"Initially we didn't know that a mutated form of a common bacteria was responsible, so during delivery the babies would get covered in this bacteria, or they swallowed it directly while breastfeeding."

"So now that you have identified the bacteria, how do you plan to stop it?"

"We haven't figured that out yet. We are hoping that Mr. Marshall's children will be born with an immunity that will be passed on to their children also."

"Is there a possibility that the bacteria might mutate again and start killing women?"

"I have no information upon which to give a scientific response to that question. I can't say whether it will or will not happen because we simply don't know at this time."

"So are you saying that with regard to the idea of Mr. Marshall having offspring with thousands of women from all over the world, it is just an experiment and the result is not guaranteed?"

"Based on current scientific knowledge we expect it to be successful, but I cannot give any guarantees."

"Dr. Samuels, we have heard testimony that women are carriers for the bacteria which for some reason unknown to us does not attack women. Isn't it true that immunity can only be passed on to the child from its mother?"

"Yes, as a general rule that is true, but because the bacteria is only harmful to males, we believe that there is a genetic component. We believe that Mr. Marshall's resistance to the bacteria will be transferred via genetic code, so his first male child will already be immune to the bacteria."

"How sure are you that this is what will happen?"

"We are not one hundred percent sure, but based on current scientific knowledge, we believe that this is what will happen."

"Thank you Dr. Samuels. At this time the defense would like to call Mr. Tyrone Marshall to the stand."

Tyrone is sworn in and Jennifer asks him: "Could you state your name and occupation for the record please?"

"My name is Tyrone Marshall and I'm a handyman, but unfortunately the federal government is preventing me from working at this time."

"Now, Mr. Marshall, we're all familiar with your case from previous testimony. But let me ask this, how do you feel about being used as a human guinea pig to rapidly increase the male population?"

"I think it's wrong to force me to do something I find morally objectionable, and should it be done I would consider it rape and I would fight against it with all my strength."

"Now, we heard expert testimony that you are using your unique position to get sweet revenge for your wrongful imprisonment, is that true?"

"Not at all, the people who were responsible for my wrongful imprisonment are dead. I have no hard feelings against anyone, rather, I feel sorry for the many women worldwide who have lost their husbands."

"What about brother in-law marriage, why are you not willing to practice something that is clearly a Bible teaching?"

"Well, I have listened to the explanation of the sociologist and I have to say that people have seriously misunderstood what brother in-law marriage is. First of all, the law applied only to ancient Israelites and had to do with preserving and keeping land inheritance within the family. Secondly, it only applied to a close family member, ideally a brother or a close male relative. Ancient Israel was a theocracy, a nation that was governed strictly by adhering to God's law. We no longer live under that system, Christians live in all parts of the world under secular governments and God expects us to obey the laws of those countries."

"But Mr. Marshall, worldwide the governments have changed the laws to compensate for this tragedy that has come upon us. Those changes are meant to be temporary, just like the brother in-law marriage arrangement, why not cooperate with the government?"

"As I mentioned before, brother in-law marriage served a specific purpose and was mandated by God himself. In a secular society that doesn't live by God's laws, such a major moral deviation without input from God is not acceptable.

Besides, the Constitution clearly states that no law can be passed in favor of or to support any religious group."

"Thank you Mr. Marshall, the Defense rests."

"Would the prosecution like to cross examine?"

"Certainly your honor. Mr. Marshall, when were you baptized?"

"I was never baptized".

"But you say you are a Christian."

"I abide by the Christian faith, but I'm not baptized."

"Okay, so what Church do you attend?"

"I don't go to Church."

"So how do you practice Christianity without being baptized or going to a place of worship?"

"I read my Bible and I pray, I learned to do that when I was wrongly incarcerated for ten years."

"Okay Mr. Marshall, let's move on. You mentioned that Christians live all over the world under secular governments, and that the Bible says that you should obey these governments. The government is making a special exemption to save the human race. They are not legalizing or promoting immoral and irresponsible behavior. Special provisions have been put into place to make sure that any children you procreate outside your marriage would be well taken care of. And this arrangement is for a limited time, only eighteen years. What is so wrong with putting your personal interests aside to obey the government? Didn't you yourself say that God expects you to obey the Governments?"

"If I were to have children with women from all over the world, according to the law, they would be raised in those countries and under those laws. They would practice the religions and customs of their mothers, and in most cases those beliefs would clash with those of the Christian faith. I cannot do that in good conscience. There's a reason why God restricted brother in-law marriage to a brother or a close male relative who was also from the nation of Israel. In fact, God prohibited the Israelites from marrying people from other nations unless they converted to Judaism."

"Okay, fair enough, but what if all those women were selected from the Christian faith?"

"Regardless, in this day and age, the decision would be mine, and I don't feel comfortable breaking a law that was re-established by Jesus Christ himself. If God has allowed this tragedy to happen and has allowed me to survive, then there must be a reason, and without any clear instruction from him I can't violate his law. I recently got married and had an intimate relationship with a woman for the first time in my life. That's something I consider sacred, and I would not want to share it with someone who is not my wife."

"So are you ready to watch the human family die out?"
"That's a bit of an exaggeration, the population is going to decline over the next one hundred years, but after that it will level off and start to climb again. Slowly at first, but after a while it will pick up."

"But Mr. Marshall, wouldn't all those children descend from you?"
"Yes, and if I were to have children with thousands of women they would also descend from me."
"Correct, but under the Marshall Exemption laws, those children would technically not be yours. If future generations descend exclusively from your marriage with your wife, then as families die off, all property and material possessions will come to be owned exclusively by your family. So when all is said and done Mr. Marshall, your decision is based on money and power isn't it?"

"No, not true at all. Some of the girls born this year will get married to my sons. As the Earth repopulates and human society becomes more complex again, property and money will be passed on to future generations, so the wealth will be redistributed again and I won't be alive to participate anyway. I don't think you have anything to worry about, mankind will be well represented. Who knows, maybe the gradual increase in the population will give the Earth time to heal from all the harm we have caused it."

"Don't you think that by limiting repopulation to your marriage you are putting humankind at risk of extinction, including your own family? What if there's an accident, another outbreak, a natural disaster? Wouldn't it be better to have children in other parts of the country and the world who would be able to survive and carry on the human race?"

"That's a possibility, but those things could still happen regardless. And when all is said and done, what I do with my body is my business, the government has no right getting involved."
"No more questions your honor."
"The witness may step down. Let's take a fifteen minute recess and then we can come back for closing arguments".

Chapter 10 – Closed door

The fifteen minutes flew by quickly as everyone returned to the courtroom. Genevieve is first up.

"This has been a very difficult period for us as humans. In less than a year, the male population of this planet has gone down to almost zero. Mass funerals became the order of the day, but amidst all the sadness and tragedy, we have adapted and we are rebuilding. The rebuilding that we do though cannot and should not be done in vain. As women, we have taken over the reins of a formerly male dominated society, and we have kept the machine going. We had to humbly admit that, without men, the legacy of what we have achieved in the face of this tragedy would be lost... forever. All the hard work that we have achieved to stabilize society and bring back order is in danger of coming to naught. Why? Because the one man who has the key to our future is blinded by revenge. And though he cites the Constitution, we know the Constitution was not designed or intended for situations like this one. When soldiers put on the uniform of this country and go to war, they know that they may not come back alive. But they do it anyway to defend this country, the Constitution and all that we represent. And even though they know that they might not return alive, they are willing to go anyway, because they know that the majority will return. They know that their children will grow up in a free society and have access to all the things that some take for granted. Those who leave wives and girlfriends behind know that if they don't return, the love of their life will end up with someone else. And yet, they make the sacrifice anyway... the ultimate sacrifice. If soldiers are willing to give their lives for this country, why should one man not give some genetic material for the sake of all humankind?"

Genevieve stares at Marshall as she walks back to her seat, then Jennifer rises from her chair slowly and begins to address the judge. "Prior to 1967, it would have been illegal for me to marry Mr. Marshall here in the State of Georgia or in any southern state. In that year, in the famous case of Loving v. Virginia, the Supreme Court ruled that it was unconstitutional for States to prohibit interracial marriage. Since then, some of the most talented and beautiful Americans have come from mixed race families. The architects of the Constitution new perfectly well what they were doing when they drafted our Constitution. They realized, based on the experience of their ancestors who came here from Europe, that without the protection of a permanent Constitution, the way would be paved for atrocities and human rights violations under the pretext of the 'common good'. One of the things that people often forget is that the Constitution doesn't give us rights. Rather, the Constitution recognizes certain basic human rights that should not be taken away under any circumstances, and it protects those rights. So what we have are Constitutional Guarantees."

Jennifer takes a quick look around the court, then she turns her body to look at Genevieve.

"The prosecution says that Mr. Marshall should ignore his 1st and 14th Amendment Guarantees and do what the government says, but to what end? Perpetuating families that are not his own. What would that involve? If a woman is an atheist, then she will raise her child as an atheist, and that child will more than likely promote or encourage laws that are prejudicial to the kids from Mr. Marshall's marriage that are raised as Christians. The whole point of having children is to raise them with and teach them your system of values, because you believe that it is the best way to live, even if others don't agree with you. If a woman from a country that has extremist elements hostile to the United States gives birth to and raises a child with Mr. Marshall's help, then there is a possibility that she or others could teach him to hate the United States. Just the thought of bringing such a child into the world makes you shiver. The world we live in has had many problems for centuries, and unfortunately, in spite of our technological advances, the problems only seemed to increase. Blame it on a formerly male dominated society if you want, but when all is said and done, we supported that system. We didn't make a difference, rather, we helped to perpetuate that system. Climate change, pollution, drug use, pornography, human trafficking, the list goes on and on. And some of those things we didn't prevent or legislate against, in the name of conserving free speech. Now the government is saying, 'we want Mr. Marshall to have children all over the world so that we can perpetuate this same system'. Why?" Jennifer asks, as she looks at the audience and then turns to look at the judge.

"An individual's desire to have a child is not a right, because one person can't make a child. A couple can choose to exercise the right to have children, or they can choose not to. Some people live their entire lives without ever getting married or having children. They write a Will and leave all their material possessions to their pets, a relative or some charitable organization. We don't force those people to have children, we respect their wishes. They trust the rest of us to use the planet's resources wisely and to raise our children properly. Their legacy will live on in us if we make the right decisions. A person's desire to have children and perpetuate their progeny is a strictly personal decision and does not supersede the right of another individual to **decide** who they want to have children with. That would be rape, plain and simple. The prosecution used a very interesting analogy about a soldier making the ultimate sacrifice so that others can live a good life. All is not lost. The Peruvian and Brazilian governments have changed their laws, and are cautiously reaching out to the isolated tribes in the Amazon, without making actual physical contact. The Indian government is doing the same with the isolated tribe on that island close to India. Our talented scientists at the CDC are working night and day to develop a vaccine and a drug that will actually trigger an immune reaction in females to kill the problem bacteria. Because we live in a free society, Mr. Marshall's sons may end up not sharing his opinion and decide that they want to have children with women from all over the world. Instead of trying to force Mr. Marshall to go against his conscience and the Constitution, the government and society in general should be doing everything possible to support his decision and create an environment in which his children can grow, flourish, and continue mankind's legacy. We have before us an excellent opportunity to discard the things that made life miserable, change the things that were supposedly imposed on us by a male dominated society, and put in place the moral foundation for a better society. Thank you."

"Okay" the judge says "court is adjourned until nine AM tomorrow morning, I will give my ruling at that time."

When Jennifer and Tyrone get home, they head straight for the kitchen. The pregnancy is causing her to get hungry very often, and Tyrone just loves to watch her eat. As soon as she is done chewing a bit of food, she washes it down with some orange juice and Tyrone just cannot resist leaning over to kiss those pink lips.

Tyrone isn't that hungry, he's trying to eat healthier anyway. Since leaving prison and heading to the CDC, he has lost some weight, and he's trying to lose a bit more. After eating something light he heads to the bedroom to check the computer. The notification that grabs his attention is from Zoe Chandiram. "Great job today Jennifer, I'm praying for you guys, hang on in there Tyrone, we're root'n for ya."

Tyrone smiles as he moves on to the next notification of interest. "Hey babe, come look at this quick!"

Jennifer who was on her way to the bedroom anyway stops by the computer and takes a look.

"The poll numbers have changed" Tyrone says, sounding very excited. "It's now split 50/50 across the entire planet!

Jennifer looks on and cracks a small smile, but she doesn't seem as enthused as Tyrone.

"I'm going to start working on the appeal."

"The appeal?" Tyrone asks. "The judge hasn't even ruled yet!"

Jennifer sits down in the EZ chair and opens up her laptop, before looking over at Tyrone. "Trust me on this one, you're not coming home tomorrow evening, and the sooner I file an appeal with the Court of Appeals the better. I'll prepare it right now and as soon as she rules I'll fill in the blanks and submit it electronically."

Tyrone was taken aback by Jennifer's comments. He immediately felt sorry for her, pregnant and fighting his case, rather than sitting back and enjoying her pregnancy. Slowly he walks over to her and kneels beside the EZ chair, she turns to look at him and he allows himself to be silenced by those big bluish green eyes. The silence comes to an end as he says: "Jennifer, I never stopped thinking about you. Even after you couldn't help me stay out of prison, I lost hope of marrying you, but I always admired you. Whatever happens I want you to know how much I love you."

A tear rolls down Jennifer's face and they kiss. When Tyrone's knees eventually begin to hurt, he rises up and heads back over to the computer as he runs his fingers through Jennifer's beautiful carrot colored hair.

The next day, Tyrone and Jennifer sit in court holding hands as the judge emerges from her chambers and the courtroom goes through the formalities. The judge begins to speak: "Every now and then a judge has to listen to a case that has no legal precedence. When we make a decision people often say we make new law, but the judiciary doesn't make new law, that belongs to the legislature. What we do is apply existing law in a new way. In this case, the legislature has already passed new law, so my job is relatively easy now. A threat to the survival of the human race is not an everyday occurrence. No laws are ever written with clauses that apply only to an alien invasion, or anything that could be pulled from the pages of a science fiction novel. Yet here we are living such a nightmare. We have spent more than six months burying our men and dealing with the grief and impotence of not understanding fully how this bacteria works. It would be foolish and irresponsible of us to not take the necessary measures to protect ourselves. I believe the government has the right to forcibly use Mr. Marshall's genetic material to perpetuate the human race, but only under the most desperate of circumstances, and with all other options exhausted. I do not believe that we have reached that threshold yet, and I hope we never get there. The government is hereby prohibited from carrying out such action under the current circumstances. Should circumstances change, they must petition this court for a review, except if legislation is passed to set that threshold. I agree with the prosecution that Mr. Marshall represents a national security interest, so I order that he be remanded in the care of the CDC with immediate effect. I also order that any visitors be pre-approved by the CDC, with the exception of his spouse who is free to visit and spend time with him at her discretion. This case is adjourned."

There is dead silence in the court as two big, burly federal agents approach Tyrone to escort him away. The US attorney and her assistant exchange congratulatory squeezes of the hand, while Jennifer opens up her laptop and submits the appeal. She has a special protector on the screen, so no one can see what she is doing, not even the cameras; just Jennifer, because she is within two feet of her screen, and beyond that, the protector distorts the image.

Chapter 11 – Open Door

Tyrone is not handcuffed or shackled. When all is said and done he is not under arrest. Besides, the government wants his detention to be as humane as possible. The last thing they want is for the public to think that Tyrone is being treated inhumanely, like a caged animal. Tyrone for his part is calm, Jennifer already prepared him for this eventuality so he is taking everything in stride.

At the CDC, his living space hasn't changed. It's as if they were expecting him to come back. Tyrone changes out of his suit and slips into a pair of shorts and a white T-shirt, before turning on the TV. Everyone is talking about his court case. Polls indicate that worldwide 60% of those surveyed do not agree with the judge's decision, while the number is at 75% in the United States. The experts and panelists have nothing new to say that Tyrone doesn't already know, so he switches to Netflix to watch a comedy special. He could really use a laugh right now, and true to his conservative attitude and the way he was raised, he avoids the vulgar and dirty stuff and looks for something the entire family can enjoy.

Two hours later Jennifer turns up with lunch, but after seeing each other they simply melt into each other's arms without saying a word. Eventually they get around to eating. Jennifer can't go too long without eating because the little person inside her is pulling all the nutrients he or she needs to grow.

In the evening, Tyrone's mother arrives with dinner as she had promised and they all eat together. Jennifer stays until late at night, long after Tyrone's mother leaves, but she doesn't want to spend the night here. It is simply not comfortable enough for a pregnant lawyer who is in the middle of an appeal. Jennifer had slept a bit in Tyrone's arms, so the relatively short drive home would not be a problem. In a world with only one man in civilized society, and all female criminals behind bars, crime is virtually zero right now. Nevertheless, Tyrone doesn't fall asleep until he gets that call from Jennifer to say that she arrived home safely.

In spite of his captivity, Tyrone sleeps like a baby. He doesn't feel like exercising today, so after speaking to Jennifer he has breakfast, watches a little TV and then changes into a shale grey sweat suit before putting on his favorite music. Soon he receives a call.
"Mr. Marshall, you have a visitor heading to you right now."
"Thanks."
Tyrone wonders who it could be, and a few minutes later there is a knock on his door. As soon as Tyrone opens the door, the fragrance reaches in and envelopes his soul in a captive embrace, preparing his mind for the image of Zoe that is slowly being burnt into his retina.
"Hi Tyrone", Zoe says as she steps forward and gives him a brief hug. But one hug was enough for her to deposit her pheromone camouflaged as designer perfume onto him. The perfume impregnated his skin and clothing, but what impacted him even more was feeling her soft body in his arms, because his automatic reaction was to return the embrace.

The uncomfortable silence that prevailed as they both looked at each other smiling was what caused Tyrone to invite her in. Tyrone is a bit surprised by Zoe's visit, so he sits in the middle of the sofa instead of to one side, making it clear that he doesn't want her to sit beside him. But Zoe was obviously not interested in sitting beside him because she has already seated herself in the EZ chair across the room and to his right.

"How did you get in?" Tyrone asks.

"I called and asked and they took my information, then they asked me to bring a picture ID with me for the visit. It also helped that you made me your first Facebook friend, and I'm also your biggest supporter."

"Not to mention that you're one of the richest and most popular women in America."

"True, but this time I think I got in based on merit and not through connections. But I have only myself to blame, in a previous life I didn't set the best example."

"Well at least your making things right, that's what counts."

"Yes, losing my father and my brothers was a big wake-up call. I still can't believe it, this world has changed so much in less than a year. Where's Jennifer, I expected her to be here?"

"She wanted to sleep at home and get some things done, she should be here in the late evening."

"Ok, so what are your plans for the day? I really don't want to intrude on your privacy, I just wanted to come here in person to give my support."

"Nothing planned really, watch TV, talk to Jennifer, watch more TV."

They both laugh.

"Tyrone... I support you guys one hundred percent, but, I have to admit that I'm still scared. The government raised some really good points and... all I'm trying to say is that... make sure you guys are doing this for the right reason. Think about it carefully and... think about whether or not you could be a bit more flexible."

Tyrone looks at Zoe straight in her eyes, all this time he has been avoiding eye contact. Her clear hazel eyes contrast very well with her very light brown skin, and her hair is dark at the roots, but gradually turn to light brown as it nears the ends. Zoe is even prettier in real life, like a movie star from a Bollywood production. She is wearing a white dress that hides her cleavage and goes halfway down her shins. Her clothing isn't tight and pressed against her body, but even then it's hard for her to hide her beautiful figure. Her skin does not have a single blemish, and she is not even wearing makeup, except for some light lip gloss. Tyrone feels a little less trusting of Zoe now, and she can read his body language very well.

"Tyrone, I know what you're thinking, and with the reputation I've had I can't blame you for thinking that. But let me assure you Tyrone, I'm genuine. The life I used to portray on Social Media was just for kicks, to be famous, to get likes. I was never a bad girl, you know how strict Indian families are. My Dad would have killed me out of shame if I had done anything immoral or indecent. Dig up any old pictures you want off the Internet, I might have been acting silly and living like a spoiled brat, but I was always with a group of **friends**, especially females. No one has ever linked me to a relationship with any guy, the only thing they criticized me of was being a spoiled brat, which I wasn't. But I was Daddy's little girl, and I got special treatment. So at twenty six years old I'm still a virgin, and proud of it. But some people don't believe me because they think that being rich and acting goofy automatically means that you sleep around. Believe it or not Tyrone, you and I have more in common than you think. My mother suffered a lot when she was younger because she was the result of a relationship between an Indian man and a black woman. If she had been born in India, it would have been virtually impossible for her to meet much less marry my dad. She went to Miami to visit some friends and by chance she ran into my dad at an Indian restaurant. The rest is history", Zoe says as she smiles with melancholy in her eyes and looks down at her hand.

Tyrone can see a tear roll down her cheek, and he can feel the silence enveloping the room. But he is not sure what to say, this has all been so sudden.

"You know, some people have criticized me for using Facebook to put myself in a good position to get close to you for selfish reasons. That was never my intention, but I have to be honest, as the debate goes on, my position has softened a bit."

"So what is your position right now?"

"Well first of all let me say that I respect your position. It's your body and I respect what you choose to do with it. I will respect and defend your decision like a true friend, but… for someone like me who is also an adherent to the Christian faith, a virgin, someone who holds to the same principles that you do. I would not object to having children for you, because let's face it. Your grandchildren are going to get married to their cousins anyway. Why not have children with carefully selected women from different countries who also adhere to the same faith. It's not something you would do forever. That's how Noah and his family started out after the flood, but his grandchildren had to get married to their cousins, otherwise the world population would never have grown. In fact, we all descended from one couple, Adam and Eve. Cain and Abel had children with their sisters. It might seem disgusting to us today, but they didn't have a choice then. It was only temporary anyway until the gene pool got bigger and other options became available, but it worked out well."

Tyrone sighs deeply as he leans back and looks up at the ceiling. "Tyrone, please don't think that I came here to represent my own interests. This is not about me. I can understand you not wanting to have children who will grow up practicing another faith, but what about the faithful Christian women all over the world? Why should they not have children who will grow up practicing the same principles that you value? Your own children or grandchildren could be at risk if there isn't a population of trained professionals around to look after their needs. You know what, maybe you're right. This world is so messed up, maybe God wants us to start over from scratch using your family as a base. I don't know, this is just too much. I think I should leave, please give my regards to Jennifer. I really love you guys and I think you make a wonderful couple. It's just that this situation is so… so weird, so stressful. Whatever decision you make, I'll support you one hundred percent." Zoe rises gracefully without looking directly at Tyrone and he stands up also, just like his mother taught him to be respectful to a woman. He wants to hug her so badly but now he's doubting his own feelings. Zoe is so beautiful, and Tyrone feels confused because he thought that what he felt for Jennifer he could never feel for anyone else, yet here he is going over every curve on Zoe's body with his eyes.

Zoe looks up at Tyrone and he looks away in shame, thinking that somehow Zoe can see his internal conflict right now. "Thanks for coming Zoe, this has been a very difficult time for everyone. I'll think about what you said. I want to do what is right, I don't want to hurt anyone, but I have to follow my conscience. I've prayed about this and God hasn't revealed anything new to me, so, I'll just have to wait."

"Thank you for your time Tyrone, you're a true gentleman. Bye." With that she lets herself out and heads down the hallway. Tyrone looks out the doorway and down the hallway with only one eye showing, but she never looks back, and he doesn't stop looking at her swaying hips until she disappears around the corner."

Tyrone has a lot to think about. He hardly eats anything and he spends his time in bed looking at the picture of him and his wife that he has on his cell phone as he plays back everything that has happened over the past week in his mind. When the door opens later he jumps out of bed, because he already knows who is coming in.

"Hi babe!" Tyrone says, as Jennifer closes the door behind her.

She smiles at him, but then she stops and sniffs the air. As soon as she looks at him with a serious face he says: "Zoe was here."

Jennifer's mouth opens wide and Tyrone smiles. He goes over to her and hugs her before planting a kiss on her lips. He then leads her to the sofa where he sits down and leans her back in his arms, with the top of her head just below his chin.

"Jennifer, I'm scared. At first I thought I was sure about what I'm doing, but now I'm not so sure."

"What did she say to convince you?"

Tyrone pauses, "you think she convinced me?"

Jennifer raises herself up, then turns around to face him.

"What did she say to convince you that you are not sure of your decision?"

"She raised some points from the Bible that I didn't have the answer for."

"Like?"

"Like the point about Noah's sons repopulating the Earth with their wives. Eventually his grandkids had to marry one of their cousins because there were no other options".

"That is true, and?"

"Well according to her I have many options, there are millions of women on the planet who are Christians."

Jennifer pauses and looks into Tyrone's eyes, and he looks back at her, searching for an answer.

"How strong is your faith Tyrone?"

"My faith? My faith in what, you, God?"

"You said under oath that you adhere to the Christian faith, even though you are not baptized or go to Church. How strong is that faith?"

"I don't know, but it's being tested right now."

"Exactly!"

"I don't get it", Tyrone says, "what are you trying to say?"

"Tyrone, you told me that in prison you had the opportunity to read the Bible several times right?"

"Right".

"When people like, Joseph, Job, David, Daniel and others were being tested, did they know why they were being tested?"

"No".

"But what did they do?"

"They held on to what they believed, their faith proved to be strong."

"Exactly!"

"So you're saying that my faith needs to be strong?"

"Well, you can't prove anything unless you test it right?"

"That's right" Tyrone responds.

"So do what Joseph, Job, David and Daniel did. Unless God points you in a different direction, do what his written law says. People often feel that if God doesn't say anything, then it means they need to make their own decision. God isn't operating on our timetable, we're operating on his. We shouldn't expect him to make a press release each time something happens in our corner of the Universe. His word is already there for us to follow, let's follow it until he decides to get involved."

Tyrone smiles as Jennifer's explanation massages his brain and puts him at ease. "I never figured you as the religious type Jennifer, I am surprised, I really am."

"Like you, I stay far away from organized religion, but I do believe in God."

"So who made you have such a strong faith, your mom or your dad?"

"Like I said my parents were a strange pair, drinking and arguing seemed to be their favorite pastime. But when I got older I started to look at things differently. The truth is, they probably didn't drink that much, but, living in a trailer park and having to deal with their arguments all the time made me stay at school for as long as I could. I always wondered why an Irish family from Boston moved to Atlanta Georgia, and after doing a little research I suspected that my Dad was molested in the Catholic Church. There are too many coincidences."

"What? You're not kidding are you?"

"No I'm not" Jennifer responds, "I think my mother with all her faults was the only true friend he had, until he died two years ago."

Jennifer's eyes fill with tears and Tyrone pulls her in close to give her a hug.

"You know what Jennifer, when I read the Bible in prison, I learned that even the nation of Israel had some bad kings who didn't follow the law. Those dudes were bad, terrible! Even in Jesus's day the religious leaders were corrupt, and they even plotted to have him killed. But you know what, if there's one thing I've learned from the Bible, it's the fact that there are always individuals who will continue to do the right thing, even if the leaders don't."

"Very good Mr. Marshall, now apply what you just said to your case. Regardless of what a judge might say, you have to follow your conscience. Because in the end, you will have to answer to God. If you follow your conscience

and you are mistaken, he will not hold it against you. But if you go against your conscience and give in to peer pressure… you're going to have a problem."
"Well said Mrs. Marshall, well said. Have I told you how much I love you?"
"Only every day, but who's counting?"
They both giggle like two teenagers as they embrace each other tightly. Then Tyrone asks the question: "What's the first thing that came to your mind when I told you Zoe was here?"
"That she came here to try and get you to change your mind."
"Were you jealous?"
"No, I trust you."
"Really?"
"Yes".
"So why do you trust me so much?"
"A woman walks into the bedroom of her thirty year old son and gives him advice, and he accepts it like an obedient preteen. That says a lot. I've seen the way you treat your Mom and your cousin. You were brought up the right way, that's not very common these days. Also, you don't hide your feelings very well, you're so innocent and noble that when you find yourself in an uncomfortable situation your body language gives you away. And the icing on the cake is, ninety nine point nine percent of the men I knew would have jumped on the opportunity to have a child with as many women as possible without having to pay child support. You're a unique person Mr. Marshall, and I'm glad you're mine, all mine". Tyrone is moved by Jennifer's words and they both dissolve into a kiss.

A few hours later Jennifer has to leave and Tyrone says goodbye. Ten minutes after she leaves there is a knock on his door and he opens it to see the president of the United States standing in front of his door dressed in a black, cotton, sweat suit.

"What up bro?" The president says as she puts her fist out to do a fist bump. Tyrone can't believe his eyes as he slowly raises his fist to greet the president.
"So are you going to invite me in or do I have to get a court order?" She bursts out laughing as she delivers a fake punch to his abdomen. "I'm just kidding bro", this she says as Tyrone steps aside to let her in, but she signals to her bodyguard that they should stay outside. Tyrone closes the door and realizes she is heading for the sofa so he settles in the EZ chair.

"Bro, we've come a long way. A black female president, and millions of white women wanting to have your baby. You got it going on!"

Tyrone smiles at her comment and then says: "All of this must be foreign to you, because you're only half black, and you grew up in a white neighborhood and went to private school."

"Ooh, someone has been reading up on me, STALKER!" They both laugh as the president stretches out in the sofa. "Is this how we're spending our tax dollars? Nice! But going back to what you said, yes, I'm half white. And just like Obama that's how I won the presidency."

"Not to mention the Indian vote, your maternal grandmother was from India. Came here as a student and married your grandfather who was African American."

"I'm impressed Tyrone, I don't know whether I should kiss you or hire you."

Tyrone looks at her with a serious face.

"You know I'm kidding right?"

"I had my doubts" Tyrone replies.

"Don't flatter yourself Mr. Marshall, I'm in my fifties, my baby making days are over."

"And for your friend they have just begun."

The president pauses and stares at him with a serious face.

"I wasn't sure, but you just confirmed it. Her father contributed to your campaign, he's Indian, you're part Indian, it makes sense."

"I'm not sure what you're talking about, I didn't confirm anything, but let's change gears a bit. Are you ready to see the human race die out Tyrone?"

"No, that's why I've done my part".

"Very funny Tyrone. I see your wife has filed an appeal to the Federal Appeals Court's Eleventh Circuit. How far do you guys plan to take this?"

"It depends on how far the government is willing to take it."

"Your mind is made up isn't it?"

Tyrone doesn't answer.

"Well, I think I've outstayed my welcome. Please give my regards to your wife. Congrats on the baby."

"Thank you" Tyrone replies.

With that the president rises from the sofa and heads out the door. Tyrone stays in the EZ chair and waits for Jennifer's call.

The next day, news about Jennifer's appeal is all over the news. But Tyrone is bored, he wants to go home to his family. Jennifer arrives with lunch and they enjoy each other's company to the full. Tyrone's mother and Desiree arrive later with dinner, and late that night, all the women leave together. As Tyrone settles into bed for the night, he Marvels at the ability of human beings to adapt and overcome adversity. It was just two or so months ago that the last male victim of the outbreak was buried, and yet, in a world that is still grappling to deal with the tragedy, women are learning to smile again. Everyone has mourned and has gotten on with their lives. Now, the focus is on the future.

The next morning, Tyrone goes to the gym to work out. All the eating and watching TV has caused him to regain a little bit of fat, so now he's taking control again. After returning he takes a shower and heads to the kitchen to make breakfast. Just then his phone rings, it's Jennifer. She's excited and screaming and Tyrone has to calm her down. The Appeals Court made a decision yesterday and she just got the notification. The lower court's decision has been reversed, and Tyrone has been ordered released immediately. Tyrone is so excited he doesn't even feel hungry anymore. Jennifer is on her way and he can't wait, so he starts walking towards the building's lobby.

Chapter 12 – Supreme Importance

How the world has changed in less than a year! The death of almost all the Earth's men brought a lot of sadness and despair. But the discovery of one healthy man, even though he was a convicted murderer, brought a glimmer of hope to the women of the world. Tyrone's second court battle in ten years proved too much for everyone. At last count, 50% of the women worldwide wanted him to have children with women from all over the world. The number was at about 75% in the United States during the Appeals Court hearing, but after that it dropped to 50% also.

A month after the Appeals Court's decision, everyone is back to living their life and putting things back in order, as society continues to recover from the loss of its men. Male prisons are empty, jails are almost empty and children are being cared for and loved liked never before. The only problem is… all the children are girls. Jennifer works mostly from home these days as she cares for the little person growing inside her. Tyrone, with the help of his cousin has learned some new skills. After starting a YouTube channel, he began to upload videos of how to do certain handyman jobs like repairing drywall, fixing a busted pipe, changing a sprinkler head etc. among many other things.

He began hiring vulnerable women who had spent time in jail and he taught them new skills. With the modified world economy and the changes in the demand and supply chain, many women all over the world had to make changes in their lifestyle. Prostitutes were suddenly left without their former source of income and had to use skills they never thought they had. Strip clubs and nightclubs closed down, and many women retrained in other professions. Unemployment has become practically non-existent.

Unfortunately, in spite of the changes, it appears that there are some women who don't want to change. For this reason, some laws have had to change to punish those women who continue to undermine society.

Tyrone's business and YouTube channel are so successful that he hardly does anything with his own hands. One woman drives while he plans the next job with his tablet and the others chip in to lift and carry stuff. They work fast and efficient, but still get paid well.

In the CDC's secret conference room, a video conference meeting has been called, and the president says to Marlene: "Okay, so what do we have on the agenda? You said this is important".

"It is Mrs. President, I think we may have found out why Mr. Marshall survived the outbreak."

"Really? Tell me more."

His mother had brought some chicken soup for him, so we started looked into the chicken soup and came up empty. However, during the outbreak, he was also taking an antibiotic. The way his mother makes the chicken soup calls for certain ingredients. Those ingredients combined with the antibiotic cause the problem bacteria to manifest a unique behavior, especially in the gut. Once they exhibit that behavior the body sees them as a threat and aggressively attacks them."

"Wow! Are you sure?" The president asks.

"We are 95% percent sure."

"When will you be 100% sure?"
"We are running some more tests, we should have an answer in 7 to 21 days."
"Okay, keep me posted, thanks Marlene."
"Thank **you** ma'am."

At the Marshall home, Jennifer has come back from her Ultrasound. Tyrone didn't
want to go, he wants to be surprised and do the big gender reveal during a Live
YouTube session. As soon as he gets home he takes a shower and puts on a light
blue T-Shirt and a pair of sweat pants. His mother and cousin are present as the
transmission goes live and there are millions of viewers worldwide. Jennifer hands
him the ultrasound and he opens it to read "likely male fetus".

There is wild shouting and celebration as his mother and cousin scream with
joy. The TV screen has been converted into a computer monitor and
congratulations begin to come in from all over the world in many languages, but
mostly English. When Tyrone's emotions get the better of him he cuddles up
beside Jennifer and hugs her while crying, his mother comes in from behind and
hugs them both.

Time passes and it's thirty days since the gender reveal. Jennifer is eating a lot, but
eating healthy, so she isn't fat. In fact, she has lost some body fat, but still shapely
and nice to look at. As she and Tyrone cuddle up in bed, she says to him: "I think
they're going to appeal to the Supreme Court."
"Why do you say that?"
"I heard from a reliable source that they are testing women with a new drug.
Apparently the drug is being made from some ingredients found in your mother's
chicken soup, plus the antibiotic you were taking during the outbreak."
"So you mean they found a cure?" Tyrone asks, with his mouth wide open.
"Apparently."
"That's good" Tyrone replies.
"Yeah, but with a cure, they can push the argument that they can now guarantee
that any children you produce will not die."
"So what do we do?" Tyrone asks.
"Let me go ask your mother what the ingredients of her soup are. Let's see if we
can tilt the scales a bit."

By the end of the week, Jennifer has completed her investigation, and she puts a post on Facebook: "So those three herbs are mild anti-bacterials, but combined, they might trigger a reaction in the bacteria and cause the antibiotic to work much better in attacking the problem bacteria in both men and women. The next day, the Internet is abuzz with excitement. The Indian government had experimented with the herbs and antibiotic immediately after reading Jennifer's post, and received very good results. The Peruvian government requested the information from the Indian's who were more than happy to share the information, and they promised that if the drug worked, they would take immediate steps to reach out to the isolated tribes in the Amazon. In fact, both the Peruvians and the Indians said that if the drug worked they would increase efforts to communicate with the tribes. The Brazilian Government then admitted that many of those tribes were living in their part of the Amazon, and that they would be willing to inoculate them by force.

Another secret meeting is called with the CDC and the president skips the pleasantries and says: "What the hell happened here? I feel like I was kicked in the gut!"

"Mrs. President, this is just as much a surprise to us as it is to you. They must be very smart to have figured this out."

"Or maybe you've got a leak."

"I don't believe so Mrs. President, they had no clue what the right proportions or combinations were. I think they just backtracked what he was doing at the time of the outbreak, looked up some information on Wikipedia and then took an educated guess."

"Whatever the case, we've lost some of our leverage. We have one man, they have several." Turning to the head of the CIA the President says: "How many isolated tribes are there anyway?"

"Let me pull up that presentation". The CIA head makes a few mouse clicks and then pulls up a graphic of planet Earth. "This is information that we pulled from Wikipedia and have been able to confirm from our satellites, spy planes and drones.

With regard to India: The Sentinelese people of North Sentinel Island, which lies right here, reject contact; attempts to contact them have usually been rebuffed, sometimes with lethal force. Their language is markedly different from other languages on the Andamans, which suggests that they have remained uncontacted for thousands of years. They have been called by experts the most isolated people in the world, and they are likely to remain so. During the 2001 Census of India, a joint expedition conducted from the 23rd to the 24 of February identified at least a few dozen individuals, but it was not exhaustive. Helicopter surveys after the 2004 Indian Ocean tsunami confirmed the Sentinelese survived, and there have been a few limited interactions with them since. Another Andamanese tribe, the Jarawas, live on the main islands, largely isolated from other peoples. They are thought to number a few hundred people.

The Tasadays in the Philippines were affected just like the rest of us, because of their contact with other Philippines.
Large areas of New Guinea are unexplored by scientists and anthropologists due to extensive forestation and mountainous terrain. The Indonesian provinces of Papua and West Papua on the island of New Guinea are home to an estimated 44 uncontacted tribal groups. Isolated tribes have been reported also in the eastern Indonesian islands. The uncontacted tribes are located in the regions of Gusawi, Lengguru, Kokiri, Derewo, Teriku, Foja, Manu, Waruta, and Brazza-Digul. However, now that a cure for the bacteria is available, I'm sure the respective governments will be stepping up efforts to reach them.

Most of the isolated people in Bolivia have had some sort of contact with the outside world, even if it is through other tribes, but we believe some males have survived in isolated family communities, although reports are still coming in. But Peruvians and Bolivians are very close, so expect the Peruvian government to reach out to them and work with them instead of working with the Gringos.

In Brazil, there are about 10,000 people in uncontacted tribes, but because of the contamination that can come in from loggers and traders who speak the dialects, we believe that only the most aggressive tribes have survived. And with the Brazilian government's plan to forcibly inoculate, we can forget about striking any deals with them.

In Colombia, very few tribes remain uncontacted and only because of their hostility. They probably number around 300, but I'm sure the guerillas will be making their own vaccine and reaching out to them, maybe even by force.

In Ecuador, the uncontacted bands or nuclear families belonging to the Taromenane and Tagaeiri tribes were located in and around the tributaries of the Rumiyaku, Tiputini, and Curaray rivers. Loggers and Oil workers often got into skirmishes with them and many even died, but with the workers dying out, we believe that many may have gotten infected when they raided the makeshift bases to plunder what was left. The very hostile ones may have survived, but again, we believe that the Ecuadorian government is making a move to reach out to them with gifts and lands restoration. We have reports of a plan to send inoculated young girls from neighboring tribes who have made contact with the outside world as brides for the chiefs".

"Brilliant" the president replies sarcastically.

"And if we move over to the Atlantic coast, former uncontacted tribes in French Guiana and Guyana have lost all their males. In Paraguay, there remain perhaps as many as 300 Totobiegosode who have not been contacted; they belong to the Ayoreo ethnicity, which numbers around 2,000. Paraguay and Bolivia were past enemies, but in this matter I think they are united against us. After Brazil and New Guinea, Peru has one of the largest number of uncontacted tribes in the world, however, their dialects are very similar to the dialects spoken by many civilized indigenous groups, and some Peruvians have used that to talk to the tribes across valleys and rivers, without making physical contact. But we already know what the thoughts of the Peruvian government are, and there are even indigenous women leaders who now see this as an opportunity to bring about a resurgence of the Inca Empire.

Satellites have picked up a few men in the Surinamese jungle, and we suspect they are the few Akulio Indians remaining who refuse all contact with the outside world. In Venezuela, sad to say the Hoti, Yanomami and Piaroa have all lost their men, because of contact with the outside world. That's it."

"Thank you very much for your informative presentation. But basically our situation hasn't changed for the better, if Mr. Marshall doesn't change his mind what do you see happening?"

The CIA director looks around nervously then starts pointing at the world map. "This is just pure speculation, but if India can somehow convince the Andaman tribes to procreate with women on the mainland, their population will stabilize and then start growing faster than ours. In Papua and New Guinea, I think they will have an easier time reaching out to those isolated tribes."

"But isn't that like a third world country?" The president asks.

"Not really, the western half of the island belongs to Indonesia. Indonesia has a mixed economy in which both the private sector and government play significant roles. The country has the largest economy in Southeast Asia, is a member of the G20, and is classified as a newly industrialized country. Their population is also 80 percent Muslim, and even though the uncontacted tribes are not Muslim, I don't think they would have too many problems convincing those tribes to procreate with them."

"Oh crap" the president says as she looks down in disgust.

"Shall I keep going Mrs. President?"

"Sure, why not, pile on the bad news."

"The other half of the Island is very close to Australia, from a partnership and cultural point of view. So make no mistake, Australia, with a healthy and educated female population is going to do all they can to support Papua New Guinea. And, Australia is also our close ally."

"Well that's refreshing", the president says as she flashes a smile. "But don't let me interrupt, keep going."

"This vaccine obviously works, and the Indians and the South Americans are obviously a step ahead of everyone else as far as inoculating and contacting isolated tribes. However, in practical terms, here is what we can expect. The Paraguayan tribes live a simple life and do not reproduce fast. Paraguay has been one of the fastest growing economies in South America in recent decades, and almost 50% of the population is poor. With the men dying off though, and with a vaccine now available, it could cause a resurgence of the Guarani culture. Guarani is a written language and is an official language alongside Spanish. With a population growth, they would eventually dominate and take over what we now know as Argentina and Uruguay. One of the things working in Paraguay's favor is that they have an average life expectancy of 75 years, even though they are not exposed to a lot of vaccines. That means that procreating with isolated tribes may not necessarily expose those tribes to any diseases that the urban population has developed an immunity to. The isolated tribes also speak some version of Gurani, so they could be the group with the fastest growth.

With regard to Bolivia, they are like brothers to Peru, and they have a common longtime foe, Chile. With Chile's male population completely wiped out, I see Bolivia reclaiming their land from Chile to gain access to the sea, and eventually conquering all of Chile, with the blessing of their neighbors in Peru.

Peru for their part is a semi-developed country, the home of the formerly glorious and great Inca Empire. They have been in touch with the isolated tribes verbally and could use the bilingual, indigenous Peruvians to bridge the gap and reestablish an Inca Empire.

Many Ecuadorean Indians who are also bilingual could also reach out to the isolated tribes, retake land taken by the government and spread into Colombia whose indigenous tribes have practically been wiped out by the bacteria. They would also more than likely spread throughout Central America and eventually reach the USA via Mexico.

Brazil of course would have a more difficult time because its uncontacted tribes are known to be hostile. However, they have a more developed economy with lots of resources, and once they get a start they could take over the Guianas and move into Venezuela as well as the Islands of the Caribbean.

In conclusion, we have only one man. But he is healthy, he has good genes and he is vaccinated and exposed to microbes just like the rest of the population. Our population is educated, healthy and powerful from a military perspective. The only thing we would need to do to keep the USA ahead of everyone else is to make babies, lots of babies. Unlike the other countries we wouldn't have all those obstacles to deal with, we just need to get Mr. Marshall to cooperate."

"Okay" the president says as she sits up in her chair. "Here are my biggest concerns. Indonesia: They seem to have a better chance of contacting their isolated tribes and integrating as soon as possible. If they start making babies at a rapid rate, in another thirty years they could start taking over South East Asia, then eventually move into Mongolia and Russia, and then West to Europe. They could even bypass India and send families to other Muslim countries in the Middle East and Africa. Fortunately we have Australia as an ally, so I will need to speak to their Prime Minister so that together with Papua New Guinea they can act as a buffer or counter balance to Indonesia.

Now, we have always had good relations with Peru. However, we don't know what they or the Indians in Ecuador will be thinking in sixty years' time when our population is made up of mostly retirees, and they have newer generations of ambitious young men. Central American countries with an indigenous population might even want to form alliances with the people from Ecuador or Peru to conserve their land and culture. Marlene, please get everything in place to execute operation tadpole, but wait for my order."

"Yes Mrs. President". Everyone in the room looks at the president, but as she rises and walks out of the room, she says "need to know people, need to know".

The President has almost arrived at the Oval Office when the CIA director catches up to her. "Why was I not read in on Operation Tadpole?"

"Did someone make you president while I was asleep?"

"I'm the Director of the CIA, I just gave you a full report on the global ramifications of this issue. Yet it appears you have some sort of backup plan and you haven't told me anything."

"I know what I'm doing, I didn't become president because my predecessor died."

"Oh, well that's a low blow", the CIA Director replies "my predecessor died, but guess who appointed me?"

The president wrinkles her face and sighs heavily as she tilts her head to one side. "Please, don't make this about you. Operation Tadpole is a domestic matter. You know very well that the CIA has no business getting involved in domestic security matters. Your boss knows, but like I told her, need to know only. Trust me, it's for your own good."

With that the president turns around and continues walking to the oval office.

A few days later Jennifer receives what she had been expecting. Notification of the Government's appeal to the US Supreme Court.

"What do we do?" Tyrone asks.

"Now we try our case in the court of public opinion", Jennifer replies, "watch this."

Jennifer sits behind the keyboard and starts typing on Tyrone's Facebook page.

"My wife's pregnancy is going well, and our little boy appears to be growing strong and healthy. However, the Government couldn't care less. In a show of total disrespect for my wife's health, they have appealed the Appeals Court's decision to the Supreme Court. What is the Government doing behind closed doors? We have been very reasonable and have done our part to help. Based on a hunch that we developed after reviewing my medical history. We posted the information online, and many countries have developed as a result, a vaccine and a cure for the problem bacteria. We are cooperating as much as we can, yet individuals within the Federal Government continue to persecute us for personal reasons under the color of law. This is not right!"

Jennifer's comment has immediate repercussions, and by midday the Attorney General has called a press conference at her office in Washington DC, scheduled for 3:00PM in the evening.

When 3:00PM finally arrives, the Attorney General steps up to the podium and says: "Good afternoon ladies… and gentleman", as she looks at the camera.
"A few days ago we filed an appeal with the US Supreme Court in the case of US v Marshall, and we have just been notified that the Supreme Court has decided to hear the case. As Attorney General this case has my full backing, because I believe it has legal merit. This is not personal, my sworn duty is to uphold the law and the law is very clear. It might not be convenient or pleasant to the party who is the subject of this legal action, but we have to trust that our legislators knew what they were doing when they passed this law. If the citizenry does not approve of the law, then they can make this known to their legislators so that the law can be changed. However, until that happens, it is my job to make sure that the law is followed and that cases of legal merit, especially those crucial to national security, are litigated to the fullest and most reasonable extent. At this time I will not take any questions as this matter is currently before the courts. Thank you."

Tyrone and Jennifer look at each other, and with the press conference now over, the network station goes back to their studios.
"So, there you have it folks, the Attorney General no doubt addressing the Facebook post by Tyrone Marshall regarding the Government's decision to appeal the case to the US Supreme Court. In the studio with us today is attorney and international affairs expert, Carla Quiroz Cisneros. Carla has both Peruvian and US Citizenship, and is licensed to practice law in both countries. Carla, thank you for joining us."
"Thank you for having me."
"First off Carla, why now? Why has the Government decided to appeal this case after more than 60 days of saying absolutely nothing or showing any interest in the case?"
        "Well, to answer your question, I don't think the case was put to bed or forgotten. Anyone who loses an appeal in appeals court has ninety days to file an appeal with the Supreme Court. Personally, I saw this coming, but I expected it closer to the 90th day and not the 60th."
"So what do you think happened?"
"Mr. Marshall and his wife obviously did some backtracking and some research and came up with a theory as to how he survived. For the good of humankind they posted that theory online, where the scientists then took that theory and ran with it. As a result we now have a cure, but here's the situation. Prior to the discovery of that cure, the United States was the only country on this planet that has a man who

is immune to the bacteria. Other countries had men, but they couldn't touch them or go near them for several reasons, the most important reason being; they didn't want to infect them and kill them with this bacteria. Now, those countries have vaccinated women who can approach those men. In addition, the vaccinated women can now transfer that immunity to their fetus should they become pregnant. And the vaccine, while not tested with men yet, shows every sign that it will work."

"But here's the thing Carla, the Attorney General just reiterated that this case is about National Security. What does this case have to do with National Security? The United Nations has passed the **Humankind Regeneration and Conservation Treaty** and several countries have passed laws to make this treaty work. Both you and I have seen all the socio-economic changes in the world. Crime is almost zero right now, never before has humankind seen so much cooperation. The death of more than 99 percent of the world's men has been a source of shared grief, it has been a wakeup call for us to make changes, and many of those changes have come very quickly through international cooperation. Why would the US Government have any reason to believe that National Security is an issue here?"

Carla smiles as she admires the innocence of the journalist.
"You know, I remember a popular song in Spanish years ago by a Mexican singer that says: "*las costumbres son más fuertes que el amor*". What that means in English is: Traditions are more powerful than love. The developed countries of the world have a history of meddling in the affairs of developing countries and exploiting them for their resources. In recent decades, Muslims have been painted as enemies of progress and Western civilizations. People haven't forgotten that. The **Humankind Regeneration and Conservation Treaty** was not intended to last forever, and it says so in the wording of the treaty. Any country can withdraw at any time and revoke any laws passed in support of that treaty. In fact, based on the silence of the US government when the ingredients for a possible cure were released by Mr. Marshall. Some have come to believe that the US government already had the cure, and they were planning to use both the cure and Mr. Marshall as bargaining chips."

"Really?" the journalist asks.
"Yes, that is what some people believe. Do I believe it personally? I don't know, I don't have enough information to form an intelligent opinion on the matter. But what I may or may not believe is irrelevant right now. The fact of the matter is that those countries have formed an opinion based on what they perceive. That could spell trouble for the US if they refuse to share their men with us. Indonesia is a

mostly Muslim country and they have lots of men living in isolated areas, who would more than likely not have a problem procreating with women from outside their tribes. Many of the Indigenous people in South America have been educated in civilized society and speak dialects that are similar to those spoken in the isolated tribes. Within two generations they could bring the isolated tribes up to speed and procreate large families. When the American girls born this year begin to turn 80, the male population in many of those South American countries could well number into the hundreds of thousands. Imagine hundreds of thousands of healthy males that are raised and educated with the sole purpose of procreating, governing and administering the countries resources. Within a lifetime, they would surpass the United States and Canada and maybe eventually absorb our territory. Not to mention the Indonesians, they could help repopulate Muslim countries and eventually absorb Asia, Sub-Saharan Africa and Europe".

"Wow, I can see now why the Government considers this a matter of National Security" the journalist says.

Tyrone mutes the volume and turns to Jennifer: "You had this figured out all along didn't you?" But Jennifer just looks at him and smiles before cuddling his arm and turning her attention back to the TV.

The next day, the Internet is abuzz with chatter about the upcoming Supreme Court hearing and the comments made by Carla Quiroz. Jennifer is preparing her arguments for the Supreme Court hearing, but she is not losing any sleep over it. With so many cases falling off the Supreme Court's calendar, the hearing is set for just two weeks away. Soon after all the men died, the president appointed female replacements to bring the number of justices back up to nine. Many now fear that since the five new justices were appointed by the president, they would automatically vote in accordance with the administration's stance.

But time doesn't stand still. It marches on, and soon Jennifer and Tyrone are headed to Washington DC. Jennifer prefers to go by car, so they head out three days before the hearing in Tyrone's luxury SUV which he bought recently. This is the first time Jennifer has ever had to appear before the US Supreme Court, and she is a bit nervous. There is so much at stake, not only from a personal perspective, but also with respect to the future of humankind and the future of the United States.

Soon, the big day arrives, and the Justices file in and take their seats, then the case is called up. Genevieve gets to go first as the Chief Justice addresses her.

"Miss. McTaggart, we have read your brief and the first question I would like to ask is. Why do you think the 1ˢᵗ and 14ᵗʰ amendments do not apply in this case? "First, let me say good morning to the honorable justices and all in attendance. I will begin by saying that I love, respect and value the Constitution, just like the people of the United States whose interests I represent in this job. My brief is not an attempt to sidestep the Constitution as some have claimed, and I will explain why. Let's take the First Amendment. The Government isn't establishing a religion or promoting the practice of any specific religion. Mr. Marshall claims that his religious beliefs prevent him from acting in a way that would benefit national security interests. All the Government is doing is pointing out that his own religious teachings do not in fact prohibit what the law asks him to do. In fact, the Government has been very flexible in its demands and is allowing him to only procreate with women who share his religious beliefs and values."

As soon as Genevieve finishes her explanation the first assistant justice asks: "But by referring to his religious or holy book, isn't the Government in fact prohibiting his free exercise of religion?"
"Not at all honorable justice, we need to bear in mind that the law does not specifically address religious beliefs. It is Mr. Marshall's **argument** that his religious beliefs would prevent him from complying with the law, we are simply pointing out that this is not so. For example, if someone who claimed to be a Christian refused to get a Driver's license, yet insisted on operating a motor vehicle, that person would be prosecuted under the law. That person could claim that they don't need a permit from any human authority to move about on the Earth which was created by God. However, without attempting to regulate his religious beliefs, the State can use the persons own religious doctrine to prove that they are simply being irresponsible. In the Bible book of Romans Chapter 13, one of Christianity's most notable figures, the Apostle Paul says that Christians should obey secular authorities. In fact, the founder of Christianity himself said: "pay back Cesar's things to Cesar, and God's things to God. There are many Christians who serve in the armed forces, who are willing to die for this country. The Government isn't asking Mr. Marshall to die for the country, we are asking him to give life."

The second Assistant Justice then leans over to her microphone. "But how does forcing Mr. Marshall to procreate with many women contribute to national security?"

"That is a good question, and there are many experts who have discussed this on national TV and in newspapers. There are countries that view the United States as an enemy to mankind. They hate the American way of life, they see us as evil. Their objective is to convert the entire world to their way of thinking, to their way of living. It would be very naïve of us to think that they would not seize on the opportunity a few decades down the road, when 99.99% of our female population is over fifty."

The third Assistant Justice then asks: "Isn't that wild speculation? Human society has been going through so many changes, many of them triggered by the **Humankind Regeneration and Conservation Treaty.** Why should we make a decision now about something that may very well not happen in the future? Where is the imminent threat to national security?"

As if she knew this question was coming, Genevieve flips to a page in her binder and says: "It was the great Winston Churchill himself who said: "Those who fail to learn from history are doomed to repeat it." After defeating the German Empire or the Second Reich in World War One, everyone believed it was the war to end all wars. Little did the world know that Adolf Hitler was secretly planning world domination. You would want to think that with his fanatical public speeches, his refusal to shake Jesse Owen's hand at the 1936 Berlin Olympics, his persecution of Jews, Jehovah's Witnesses and anyone else who didn't accept his ideology, that people would have connected the dots. But they didn't, and the world was caught unprepared, and we almost lost World War Two."

The fourth Assistant Justice then says: "One could argue that we have indeed learned, and that is why we have the **Humankind Regeneration and Conservation Treaty.** Never before has humankind ever agreed on anything in such a short time, and unanimously. Are you asking us to ignore the 14th Amendment and allow the Government to carry out what would essentially be rape? Wouldn't that be depriving the person of his liberty and to some extent his life"

"That is a valid concern" Genevieve replies, "but the 14th Amendment also allows the Government to suspend certain rights and privileges through "**due process of law**", and we do have laws that address that specific situation. Those laws will begin to expire 18 years from now and new laws will be passed to address the existing situation at that time, but the Constitution will remain unchanged. Once we have overcome this temporary hurdle and we begin to experience a reasonable population growth, Mr. Marshall will no longer be required to procreate with different women."

The Chief Justice checks and realizes that there are no more questions, so she thanks Genevieve who returns to her seat. Next, Jennifer is invited by the Chief Justice to approach the podium.

"Mrs. Marshall, you have heard the Government's argument regarding your client's posture, let us hear your response please."

"Thank you honorable justices. My esteemed colleague has mentioned that the Government has not passed a law regarding any religion, nor is it promoting any specific religion over another. Truth be told, the statute doesn't mention religion. But once the Government begins to interpret scripture, they are in fact violating the First Amendment in *"prohibiting the free exercise thereof"*. What if Mr. Marshall were Muslim, Hindu, Buddhist or Jewish? Would the Government then dig through those religious teachings to find an argument to get him to comply? I'm sure my point has become clear. The framers of the Constitution had well over five thousand years of human history to learn from. They knew of the quagmire that society can get into when the ruling class starts depriving people of their religious freedom, in order to enforce what they interpret to be the 'common good'."

The fifth Assistant Justice then jumps in: "So are you saying that in a case like this, the First Amendment takes precedence over the Fourteenth?"

"As part of the Bill of Rights, the First Amendment carries a lot of weight because it establishes certain guarantees that a person can never be deprived of. However, let me hasten to add that my esteemed colleague has totally misapplied the Fourteenth Amendment as it applies to this case."

"Why do you say that?" the sixth Assistant Justice asks.

"Well, the Fourteenth Amendment isn't a free pass to take away people's Constitutional Guarantees just like that. The due process clause applies to "life, liberty, or property" and is narrowly applied to persons who have been convicted of a crime and need to be incarcerated in the public interest and as punishment. In addition, the sentence before that says: "No State shall make or enforce any law which shall abridge the privileges or immunities of citizens of the United States". In effect, what this means is that no state, nor the Federal Government can pass a law that will in effect nullify an area of the Constitution, especially the Bill of Rights. The Government has made an argument in the interest of national security, but even that argument is weak. Have we not learned anything in reviewing world history? Did we not sign a treaty recognizing the errors and suicidal policies of a male dominated society? Why does the Government insist on a course of action that represents the flawed thinking of a male dominated society that no longer exists? A course of action that was causing us to deplete our planet's resources and driving us closer and closer to mutual destruction."

The seventh Assistant Justice then says: "Using that logic, we would also have to accept that the Constitution, which was drawn up by men, is also flawed and needs to be modified."

"Not at all Honorable Justice. Humankind has had sobering moments and periods where we made good progress. Unfortunately, most of those moments usually came after a period of tragedy, tragedy provoked by mankind itself. This is our sobering moment. We should seize that moment to sit down with women from other countries, even those we consider hostile to us and say: 'Hey, we almost lost everything. Let's rebuild, but not on the basis of suspicion or believing that one group of people is superior to another. Let's rebuild as a family and lay the foundation for future generations to go down a better path'. We should not be using this situation to launch a new arms race where instead of making guns and bombs in factories, the womb is used to produce elements of destruction. This is the perfect time to put in motion the things that will help us to have a future that is far different from what we had in the past. And it can be done! Every single country on this planet sat down and signed a treaty that everyone agreed on. Why aren't we building on that instead of starting a new arms race? There is no urgent national security issue that requires us to essentially rape Mr. Marshall, no, the groundwork is already in place, we just need to continue talking. My colleague mentioned that people have died for this country with the belief that those who they left behind will be taken care of. Prior to Mr. Marshall proposing marriage to me. I was resigned to the fact that I would never have children. I imagined that with all the suffering people of African descent have endured, that Mr. Marshall was probably going to get married to someone of his own race, and in time populate the Earth with only one race, with himself as the forefather. I was so wrong in my assumptions, and I'm grateful to Mr. Marshall for choosing me to be the mother of his children. Millions of women will die without ever having children, just like some soldiers go to war and never return home, never get the chance to get married or even have children. The same principle applies here. Those women who will not get the chance to have children must trust in us to keep the human race alive. They must work hard now that they are alive, to promote the values and to create the infrastructure that will guarantee the survival of the babies that will be born, even if the babies are not theirs. That is sacrifice, that is service!"

There is a deafening silence as the justices look around at each other. The Chief Justice then says: "I believe we have heard enough regarding this case. We will deliberate and communicate our decision in the usual manner. Court is adjourned."

As soon as they step out of the courtroom, Jennifer wants to eat but the media attention is just too much. As soon as they got into the car she says to Tyrone: "Let's go have lunch in Lexington Virginia, there's a restaurant there that I've heard about and I would love to visit."

Tyrone pulls up the GPS and types in Lexington Virginia.

"Baby, that's three hours away, I thought you were hungry?"

"That's fine, I've got snacks, let's go."

Tyrone smiles as he heads out of the parking lot and begins his route to get to I-66. Later on he will switch over to I-81 and take it all the way down to Lexington. Tyrone is going over the route in his head as he reorganizes his itinerary mentally. Jennifer can't sit for too long, so he's thinking of getting a hotel room in Lexington, and then leaving the next day for Charlotte North Carolina via I-81 and then I-77. That's a four hour drive, so he's thinking of staying in a nice hotel in Charlotte, and then leaving the day after for Atlanta.

During the drive, Tyrone and Jennifer talk about the case, what the Supreme Court might decide and how it would affect them.

"I think they are going to rule in our favor" Jennifer says. "I believe Roe versus Wade and other similar decisions have tied their hands, but of course, the Government is not going to give up. I'm sure they'll try and repeal the necessary Amendments or do something to have their way. I'm not worried about that though, as long as I have you by my side I'm happy."

Tyrone looks at her briefly before looking back at the road, then reaches out and holds her hand.

The couple spend a wonderful two days on the road, receiving hugs and well wishes from supporters. But there are also some who believe that they are being selfish and that they should do their part to "save" mankind.

Soon they are back home in Atlanta and Tyrone's mother is waiting for them with a wonderful, southern, home cooked meal. Barely two days pass before Jennifer and Tyrone begin to receive boxes with gifts for their unborn son. The boxes come from all over the US, and Jennifer is overcome with emotion as she perceives the support from women all over the country.

The next Monday, an officer from the Supreme Court turns up at her door and has her sign for a large envelope. Jennifer is excited and nervous at the same time. She opens the envelope which contains the Supreme Court's decision, which is relatively brief.

"After much deliberation, this court has found that the arguments presented by the defendant are in harmony with the spirit and the letter of the law, as it appears in the United States Constitution. It is our belief that the framers of the Constitution could never have imagined in their wildest dreams our current predicament. Nevertheless, we believe that the applicable Amendments were construed in such a way so as to address the most unforeseen of circumstances. In light of this fact, we have to agree that the Constitution prohibits the Government from forcing Mr. Marshall to do something that violates his moral and religious conscience. The government's concerns about national security are at best speculative and may in fact be counterproductive to the ideals and intentions of the **Humankind Regeneration and Conservation Treaty.** In view of the foregoing, we encourage the Government as well as Mr. Marshall to engage in further dialog to address their mutual concerns. This decision prohibits the government from using the Marshall Exception Act as a basis for incarcerating Mr. Marshall or denying him any of his constitutional guarantees. The decision of this court is unanimous."

Jennifer smiles with relief as she finally sits down in the sofa with a big grin on her face. After a few minutes pass she sends a text message to Tyrone: "We won!" Tyrone responds with a celebration emoji.

That evening, Tyrone and his family celebrate their victory with a feast and beautiful music, while in the White House, the president has called a meeting with her top aides.

"Ladies, Operation Tadpole is a go and will be executed a week from today. Regardless of what the Supreme Court says, I was elected by the people to look out for the interests of this great nation and secure our future. It's a tough decision, but someone has to make it and the buck stops with me. You have all been briefed with your answers for the media. Remember, total denial! If and when it comes to light, I will take the blame and say that you were all not informed of my decision. I will fall on my sword and sacrifice myself, but this great nation will live on, and two hundred years from now I will be praised as a heroine and not a villain. You are all dismissed."

Everyone leaves except for the Director of National Security. "Mrs. President, like I told you from day one, I do not support this decision. I see very bad things coming from this."

"Don't worry about it, it's all on me." This she says as she leaves the room and heads for the Oval office.

The next week, just as twilight begins to yield to nightfall, the doorbell at Tyrone's house rings. Jennifer says: "Honey, could you get that please?" As she settles into the recliner.
Tyrone opens the door and sees four very big women dressed in black suits.
"Tyrone Marshall?"
"Yes."
"Could you sign for this please sir?"
Tyrone takes the clipboard to read what he is signing for and suddenly his body goes limp. Jennifer hears what sounds like the discharge of a stun gun and says "Tyrone?" but there is no answer. By the time she gets to the door she can hear a vehicle pulling away, and she reaches the doorway just in time to see a black SUV speeding down the road. Tyrone is nowhere to be seen, and with tears streaming down her face Jennifer screams "NOOOOOOOO!"

That long and loud scream reverberated in her mind and caused Jennifer to sit upright in her bed. It's still dark outside, but almost time for her to get up anyway. As she looks around her apartment she can tell that she just awoke from a dream. She touches her flat abdomen and confirms that she is not pregnant, and there is no wedding ring on her finger. She is still a 25 year old rookie with the Public Defender's office, but what she had dreamt felt so real. Her bedsheets are drenched with sweat, and Jennifer removes the sheets and takes them to her large washing machine. She turns on the TV and confirms that what she had dreamt is not real, as there are men transmitting live on several channels. Leaving the TV on, she heads to the bathroom to take a shower, after which she gets dressed. As she heads to the coffee shop close to work, she activates the hands-free feature on her car radio.
"Call dad".
"Calling Dad" her phone responds.
"Hello."
"Hi Dad, how are ya?"
"Well this is a nice surprise, how's my little girl doing?"
"I'm fine, just calling to let you know that I love you and I'm grateful for all you did for me. Would you and Mom like to come over for dinner on Sunday?"
Jennifer's father goes silent as his face wrinkles and the tears begin to pour out of his eyes. The last time he heard such tender words from his daughter, she was six

years old. Fighting to regain his composure he says "sure dear, just let me know the address and mommy and I will be there."

"Okay, bye, see you on Sunday" Jennifer says as she hangs up, tears rolling down her face also.

Later on she walks into her office and sits down at her desk, there is a new file in her incoming tray. As she takes a sip from her cup, she reaches over and pulls out the file, she almost spits out her coffee as she reads the name on the file: **Marshall, Tyrone**.

END

Made in the USA
Columbia, SC
15 October 2022

69432907R00048